LOVE WILL FIND A WAY

Bethany Burnett isn't surprised to discover her godfather Wendel holding a garden party in the snow. What does take her breath away, though, is the presence of Sam Richards, bad-boy film director. His unexplained disappearance had fuelled media speculation for weeks at the time. Now, years later, he's back and filming a costume drama at Wendel's Jacobean manor house. When Wendel volunteers Bethany's services as Sam's assistant, she fears troubled times are ahead — and it is not long before her fears are realised . . .

MARGARET MOUNSDON

LOVE WILL FIND A WAY

Complete and Unabridged

LINFORD
Leicester

First published in Great Britain in 2016

First Linford Edition
published 2017

A catalogue record for this book is available
from the British Library.

ISBN 978–1–4448–3439–0

Published by
F. A. Thorpe (Publishing)
Anstey, Leicestershire

Set by Words & Graphics Ltd.
Anstey, Leicestershire
Printed and bound in Great Britain by
T. J. International Ltd., Padstow, Cornwall

This book is printed on acid-free paper

1

Dark clouds lumbered across the sky. It was only half past three in the afternoon, but already the light was fading from the day. In the fields, lambs huddled together for warmth. Bethany knew how they felt. Her heater was on full blast but her toes were numb with cold.

With journey's end in sight, she relaxed her grip on the steering wheel. It would be good to see her godfather again.

In his youth, Wendel Nelson had been quite a ladies' man. There had been a string of broken hearts until he fell in love with the beautiful Mary Lennox. According to family history, he'd had a battle on his hands before he won Mary's heart, but after they were married he had never looked at another woman.

Together they travelled the world. Wendel was the perfect diplomat and his wife a brilliant hostess. No one was ever turned away from any of Wendel and Mary's parties, and they made for some pretty lively occasions. After Wendel retired they retreated to the border town of Steeple Maltravers. Waterbridge Manor became their new home and they set about making their mark on the local scene.

Wendel had sounded his usual cheerful self when Bethany had telephoned, but she suspected he was putting on a brave face. He was not a new age man. Mary had done everything for him. To everyone's huge amusement, once when he had been offered a slice of fruitcake at a society wedding, he had been forced to turn to Mary to ask if he liked marzipan.

Mary's delicate health had been a source of constant concern to Wendel, and a savage bout of flu had left her too weak to leave her bed. When Mary passed away in her sleep, Bethany had been in Canada. Unable to break her private nursing contract, she had not attended the funeral. Although Wendel said he perfectly understood, it was something that sat uneasily on Bethany's conscience. Wendel had always been there for her, and she didn't like to think she had not been there for him.

Bethany's tyres lost traction on a patch of ice and she forced herself to concentrate on the road in front of her. She eased her car around the bend, and there in the distance, majestic in the fading gloom, stood the small but graceful Jacobean country house, Waterbridge Manor.

Wendel, bless him, appeared to have illuminated the garden in honour of her arrival. Fairy lights dangled from bare branches and wooden tables were decorated with Christmas candles. It made a pretty sight. Bethany wrinkled her nose. Could she smell smoke?

She slewed to a halt and wound down her window. Snowflakes mingled with the smell of hot sausages, and in the background someone was playing party music at a headache-inducing level. Even by Wendel's standards, this was over the top. It was then Bethany noticed that the garden was full of people.

'Bethany, my Angel,' Wendel boomed. Larger than life, he strode towards her car and opening her driver's door, dragged her to her feet and enveloped her in a bear hug. 'Where have you been?'

'Wendel?' Bethany returned his kiss in stupefied confusion. 'What's going on?'

'We started the party without you, I'm afraid. Everyone was so hungry they refused to wait any longer. I'm glad you're here — now I can get things going in earnest.'

Bethany struggled free from Wendel's embrace. 'Are you having a garden party?'

'We are indeed.'

'It's February.'

'We don't need strawberries, do we?'

'But it's snowing.'

Wendel brushed aside her concern as if it were of no importance. 'Don't worry about that. Nothing a pair of boots and a coat won't put right. We'll soon have you warm. Now come and meet everybody.'

'Hi,' a man wearing a checked shirt

under a huge quilted jacket introduced himself, 'Johnny Morton at your service. Would you like me to relieve you of your rabbit?' He peered into the back of Bethany's car. A quivering pink nose poked through the wire mesh of a hutch and sniffed Johnny's fingers. 'A Giant Papillon, if my eyes don't deceive me.'

'I didn't know you had a rabbit,' Wendel said.

'I made arrangements to adopt a rescue rabbit before I went to Canada,' Bethany explained. 'You don't mind an extra guest, do you?'

'Not at all. The more the merrier.'

'The poor old chap must be in sore need of a comfort break. My kid sister is very into rabbits. I know exactly what to do,' Johnny assured Bethany. 'What's his name?'

'He doesn't have one. I've only just collected him.'

'Never mind. I'm sure we'll bond.'

'Who is that?' Bethany hissed as Johnny manhandled the travelling hutch off the back seat.

'First cameraman, I think,' Wendel said. 'Actually, I'm not too sure of his correct title. If you're that interested, I daresay he'll put you right later. Let's get you kitted out in some warm clothes, then I'll perform the introductions.'

The music grew louder as she and Wendel approached the house. 'We couldn't transfer the sound system into the garden so we upped the volume,' Wendel explained as he retrieved a garden coat off a hook in the utility room and produced a pair of sturdy boots. 'These should do. Look, there's even a woolly hat in the pocket.' He rammed it over Bethany's springy blonde hair.

She wrinkled her nose. 'Where on earth has it been?'

'I have absolutely no idea. Haven't seen it for years. No matter.' Wendel gave an airy wave of his hand. 'Who cares as long as it does the job?' His craggy face broke into a beaming smile. 'You look as lovely as ever, my darling.' He stroked her face with the pads of his thumbs. 'I'm so glad you're here, and you're to stay as long as you like.'

'Wendel — ' Bethany was forced to raise her voice above the music.

'Yes?'

' — what are all those people doing on your lawn, and who are they?'

'Good question. This fine young man — ' Wendel grabbed the arm of a passing guest. ' — is the Honourable Hugo de Montchapelle.'

Bethany raised her eyebrows. He certainly had the looks to go with the title.

'He's only a second son, so it's no good setting your cap at him, my darling. Anyway, he's engaged to Miss Elena Wick-Stanley. She's the daughter of Sir Henry Wick-Stanley. Hugo's mother is French and a bit of a handful, if you get my meaning.' Wendel tapped the side of his nose and winked.

Hugo grinned, revealing perfect white teeth. 'There's no need to look so surprised. Wendel's not being rude about my family,' he explained. 'He doesn't know my mother. My real name is Anthony

Granger. Hugo de Montchapelle is only my character.'

'Character?'

'*Love Will Find a Way.*' Anthony was still smiling.

'Look, could we start again?' Bethany pleaded.

'Hello, are you the guest of honour?' A cheerful middle-aged lady kissed her on the cheek. 'Lovely to see a fresh face, although I expect by the end of the shoot we'll be sick of the sight of each other. Continuity is my bag.'

Bethany was beginning to feel as if she had passed into an alternate reality. Either that or she was overtired. Nothing was making any sense.

'Let's get some food inside you,' Wendel insisted. 'You'll feel better after you've eaten something.'

'Have some of this to warm you up.' A cup of hot soup was thrust into Bethany's hands.

'Where would you like me to put your rabbit?' Johnny Morton was back. 'He's had a drink and nibbled on some lettuce and his other needs have been seen to.'

'I'm sure he'd like to join the party. Put him in the conservatory for the moment — if that's all right with you, Angel?' Wendel looked at Bethany.

'As long as no one lets him out.'

'Actors don't like being upstaged by children or animals,' Johnny assured Bethany, 'so he'll be perfectly safe. No one will ask him to dance.'

'Are you warm enough?' Wendel put a hand under Bethany's chin. 'You're rather pale.'

Bethany's toes now tingled with warmth in her garden boots. She looked into Wendel's weather-beaten face. 'I've never felt better,' she was forced to admit, and squeezed his hand. 'And you?'

'I'm good too.'

'But you're going to have to explain what's going on,' Bethany insisted. They settled down on one of the wooden seats.

'*Love Will Find a Way.*'

'That's what Anthony said, and it's not the answer I was looking for.' The tomato soup scalded Bethany's lips.

'It's a costume drama,' Wendel explained.

'And you're entertaining the crew to a party in the snow?' Bethany still wasn't sure she had grasped the situation.

'Have one of these.' Wendel thrust an onion-laden burger into Bethany's hands while a passing Anthony relieved her of her empty soup cup.

'You haven't taken up acting, have you?' Bethany asked Wendel with a note of alarm.

'No. It's Waterbridge Manor that's taking on the starring role. The old girl is playing the lead.'

'They're filming here?'

'I've been told the house is exactly right for the interior shots, and they particularly wanted to use this area for the exterior shots — the market and all that.'

Steeple Maltravers had been granted a market charter in 1330 by Edward III. A cross now signified all that was left of the square, as most of the community did not survive the Black Death, but Steeple Maltravers was an attractive town full of gabled buildings. Bethany supposed it was inevitable that the area would eventually attract the interest of a film company.

'There's also the roof,' Wendel admitted with a gloomy sigh.

'What's wrong with the roof?'

'Like the rest of us, it's showing its age. I've been offered an eye-watering amount for the rights to film here and I couldn't afford to turn it down. You've no idea how expensive repairs can be, especially for a house like Waterbridge Manor. The wiring is suspect too, and I haven't dared inspect all the upstairs rooms. I'm afraid of what I might find.' Wendel patted Bethany's hand. 'But enough of my problems. We're going to have the most tremendous fun — you'll see.'

'Well with all these people around, you won't be lonely. You'll hardly notice I'm here. You won't need my company.'

'Angel,' Wendel reproached her, 'I always need your company, and I shall get very cross if you ever make a remark of that nature again.'

Bethany cast him a shamefaced smile. 'I spoke without thinking.'

Wendel nodded. 'Now where were we?'

'Talking about the film. Is the entire cast staying here too?'

'No, the cast is billeted out in the village. There won't be any filming upstairs, so your bedroom hasn't been touched. I was insistent on that.'

A shadow moved towards them and bumped into the arm of their bench. Its owner frowned, as if the collision was the bench's fault, before continuing his lively telephone conversation. 'You cannot let me down now,' he barked down the line.

'Who's that?' Bethany stage-whispered.

'Sam Richards. He's the director.'

Bethany's eyes turned into saucers of surprise. '*The* Sam Richards?'

'You've heard of him? Is he famous?

He certainly acts the part. He's put me in my place once or twice. It was possibly my fault,' Wendel admitted. 'I got taken to task for talking during a shot.'

'He's new age — cutting-edge; well, he is now,' Bethany emphasised, even though Sam's last film had been over two years ago and certainly not a lightweight costume drama.

'My darling Angel, I haven't a clue what you're talking about,' Wendel replied. 'But I suppose cutting-edge is good?'

The bench vibrated as Sam Richards thumped down beside Bethany.

'Problem?' Wendel asked with a mild smile.

'My personal assistant just quit. Who are you?' He stared at Bethany.

Bethany knew her nose was glowing from the heat of the soup, and she could feel her hat slipping down over her eyebrows. She pushed it back up her forehead but it immediately slipped down again.

'Meet my goddaughter, Bethany. We call her Angel.'

'We do not,' Bethany hissed. Wendel was the only one who still called her by her childhood nickname.

'She used to adore angel cake,' he explained.

'Love the hat.' Sam raised a sardonic eyebrow. 'Even if it does smell of a scarecrow's pocket.'

Bethany longed to snatch the itchy wool beanie off her head, but she couldn't give Sam Richards the satisfaction of scoring a direct hit. For his part he looked every inch the edgy modern director. His leather jacket was unzipped, and beneath it he was wearing a thin black T-shirt embossed with a red dragonhead logo.

'Bethany is an excellent personal assistant.' Wendel leaned across her to address his next remark to Sam. 'She's also got extensive nursing experience.'

2

'Drop those sausages!' Wendel raised his voice over the disturbance emanating from a far corner of the garden. 'Excuse me.' He hared off in pursuit of a scruffy border terrier who appeared to be making off with half the contents of the barbecue.

Although snow was now falling steadily, Bethany could feel prickles of heat inching up her backbone. Flecks of snow speckled Sam's dark brown hair. The corner of his mouth quirked into a smile. 'So, you're a nurse?'

If Bethany could have described his voice in two words, it would have been *dark chocolate*.

'No, I'm not,' she corrected him firmly.

'Wendel said you were.'

'Wendel was being economical with the truth.'

'He also said you were an excellent personal assistant. Was that another economical statement?'

'No.' Bethany hesitated. 'That bit's true.'

'And you're not working at present?' Sam raised an eyebrow.

'I was outsourced,' Bethany admitted. No way was she going to admit her history with Leo and Harland Somerville. She wasn't sure Wendel knew the full details.

'What makes you think you could work on a film set?'

'I don't.'

'Wendel said you did.'

'Mr Richards . . . ' Bethany took a deep breath.

'Sam, please.'

'Mr Richards,' she continued, 'I don't know if you think you're conducting an interview, but before we go any further I need to put you straight on one or two things.'

'Can it wait?' Sam's mobile began to buzz.

'No, it can't.' Bethany snatched the mobile out of his fingers. 'They'll ring you back.' She cut the call.

'Respect,' Sam drawled. 'You've got the job.'

'Splendid news.' Wendel caught the tail end of the conversation. 'And I have been equally as successful in retrieving these.' He dangled a string of sausages in front of them.

'I'll have those.' Anthony Granger was hovering by his elbow. He snatched at the sausages. 'The troops are getting impatient.'

Wendel inspected the sorry state of the barbecue fare. 'They are rather the worse for wear. The sausages, not the troops.'

'Don't worry about that,' Anthony reassured him. 'Everyone is hungry enough to eat anything.'

'Bouncer.' Wendel now addressed the dog panting by his side. The terrier gave a gentle whine in acknowledgement of his name. 'Bethany's come all the way from Canada to see you, and so far you haven't had the good manners to welcome her home.'

A bundle of brown fur immediately launched itself at Bethany's legs and barked an enthusiastic greeting. She bent to stroke the scrubby snow-encrusted ears and earned a look of adoring gratitude.

'That dog won't be able to remain on set,' Sam grumbled. 'Catriona Cleeve's agent says she's allergic to animals.'

Johnny Morton joined the group. 'Bang goes Furry's chance of landing a leading role. The rabbit. I've christened him Furry,' he explained to a puzzled Sam. 'He's holding court over there.' Johnny pointed to a group gathered around the hutch who were busy poking small pieces of lettuce through the wire mesh. 'If you care to make yourself known to him, I'm sure he'd be gracious enough to grant you an audience.'

Bethany realised she was still clutching Sam's mobile as it began to vibrate in her hands.

'Deal with it,' Sam instructed as she tried to hand it back to him.

'Why should I?' Bethany demanded.

'Because I'm going to get something to eat.'

'They'll ring you back,' Bethany repeated her response to Sam's earlier call, hoping she hadn't offended anyone important.

'I hear you're joining us.' Johnny scooped up a wriggling Bouncer and tickled a tender spot behind his left ear. Bouncer squirmed in ecstasy.

'Nothing's been decided,' Bethany countered.

'Yes it has,' Wendel insisted. 'Johnny, any problems, Bethany will deal with them.'

'Wendel,' Bethany had another go at protesting, 'I haven't agreed to anything.'

'They're filming on a tight schedule,' Wendel reproached her. 'You wouldn't want to hold things up by being difficult, would you?'

Bethany gaped at the injustice of her

godfather's remark. 'How can any hold-up possibly be my fault?'

'Hey, gang.' Johnny deposited Bouncer back onto the lawn and cupped his hands, his breath misting the cold air. 'Listen up, I have an announcement. Can someone please turn down the music?'

The eerie silence that followed was punctuated by the softest whisper of floating snow and the crackle of charcoal from the barbecue.

'For those who haven't been introduced, meet Bethany Burnett.' Johnny grabbed her arm and held it up. His announcement was greeted with enthusiastic applause and robust whistles. 'This thoroughly disreputable band of individuals, Bethany, is the crew of *Love Will Find a Way*, a production that's going to be the costume drama of the century — isn't it?' His words were again greeted with a wild round of applause. 'Bethany has agreed to come on board, and although I know it's a decision she'll soon regret, I hope you'll all give her the usual Richards Productions warm welcome.' More whistles and cheers followed.

'Now it's your turn,' Johnny urged.

'To do what?' Bethany was beginning to feel she had been in collision with a wall that wasn't listening to her.

'Make a speech.'

'What do you want me say?'

'First thing that comes into your head.'

'Um . . . I've never attended a garden party in the snow before,' she began.

'First time for everything,' a voice called back.

'I really came to Waterbridge Manor because I was overdue a visit to my godfather, Wendel Nelson.' More whoops followed the mention of his name. 'But I seem to have been talked into a new job.'

'Way to go.' Johnny led the applause. 'Now we're ready to party.'

The music started up again and a swarm of people headed in Bethany's direction. A glass of something herbal was thrust into her hands with strict instructions to 'drink up before it gets cold'.

'Is film life always like this?' she said.

'You should see us when we really get going,' Johnny replied.

The drink warmed Bethany's frozen limbs; and as the party progressed, an army of young men, all energetic movers and shakers, invited her to dance with them. Eventually, when her legs refused to support her any longer, she collapsed on one of the garden benches. The tree lights, she noticed, were making a brave stand against the snow as the afternoon slid into evening.

Now he was no longer attached to his phone, Sam Richards began to enter the party spirit. Without exception, his crew appeared to hold him in high regard and seemed excited at the prospect of working with him.

Five years ago he had been a rising star of the motion arts industry. According to reports Bethany had read in the press, he didn't care who he upset — leading ladies, supporting artistes, motion picture moguls — as long as he got the effect he was looking for. His first two films had been box-office smash hits.

Then, with his career riding high and without warning, he disappeared from the scene. Rumours were rife — a love affair, financial issues, a nervous breakdown, even a secret marriage were hinted at. But despite the whispers, no one could discover the true reason for his disappearance. Eventually interest in Sam Richards had waned.

Now it seemed he was back and in her godfather's snowy garden, strumming a guitar and singing old country-and-western ballads that had everyone joining in. Throughout it all, his mobile hadn't stopped ringing. In desperation, Bethany had muted the ringer. If Sam wasn't worried about missed calls, then neither was she. Wendel put an arm around her shoulders.

'You're not cross with me?' he asked.

'Why should I be?'

'For volunteering your services as company nurse?'

'As long as it's nothing more serious than a sticking plaster or the occasional headache pill.'

'That's my girl.'

The garden was now almost deserted. Most of the crew had slid down the hill back to the warmth of The Goose and Galleon, and the stragglers were busy shouting goodbyes to each other. Bouncer was doing his best to warm Bethany's feet, but she was getting seriously cold and finding it difficult to move her lips.

She looked at the smouldering ashes of the barbecue and the litter of paper plates. 'I suppose we ought to clear up,' she offered with a lack of enthusiasm.

'Someone will sort the mess out in the morning. You do like Sam, don't you?' Wendel asked.

As if in reply, Sam's mobile began to vibrate. Bethany extricated it from her pocket. 'What am I supposed to do with this? Where is he?'

Wendel inspected the caller display. 'Perhaps you should answer this call. It's from the great man himself. I'll leave you to speak to him in private. When you've finished, come inside. It's getting far too cold to sit out here. I don't know what you were thinking of, attending a garden party in the snow,' he added with a wicked twinkle in his eyes.

'Hello?' Bethany waited for Sam to speak.

'We should be with you about half seven tomorrow morning.' His voice was crisp and businesslike.

'Where are you?'

'The Goose and Galleon.'

'I didn't see you leave.'

'If I hadn't moved on, you would've been stuck with most of the boys until the small hours. They know how to party and I know what I'm talking about. Get a good night's sleep. We've a busy day ahead of us tomorrow. Thank Wendel for the party.' He paused. 'And welcome to Richards Productions.'

Bethany stood up and stamped her feet in an attempt to bring some warmth back into them. She wished she'd had the courage to turn down Sam's offer, but with little prospect of finding a job in the near future, she hadn't been left with much choice.

'Bethany,' Wendel called out from the conservatory window, 'what say we have a hot drink and something on toast before settling down to watch the late-night movie?'

Bethany joined Wendel in the kitchen. 'Sam said thanks for the party and to tell you he'll be here at half past seven tomorrow morning.'

'I haven't been up that early for years,' Wendel protested.

'Then you'd better start getting used to the idea.'

'You can let him in if I'm not respectable, can't you?' Wendel smiled. 'I'll be in the lounge; there's a documentary I want to watch. It's on before the film. Bring the tea through.'

'You're going to have to stop keeping late hours,' Bethany called after him. There was no reply from Wendel. With a sigh she put two slices of toast under the grill and began looking around for the cheese.

3

Icicles dangled from the greenhouse gutter, and a magpie was using its beak to stab at the ice on the bird bowl but without much success. Bethany yawned and rubbed sleep from her eyes. Wendel had talked late into the night, recounting some of his old stories, and Bethany hadn't had the heart to stop him. He'd come alive as he retold the saga of his and Mary's experience when trying to book a room in a hotel abroad for the night.

'I couldn't make the receptionist understand why two people couldn't cope with one bunk bed pushed up against a wall in a room that was little bigger than a broom cupboard. He kept saying, 'We have carnival, no spare beds.''

'What did you do?' Bethany asked, although she had heard the story countless times.

'We decided to forget about sleep and joined the carnival instead. It was one of the best nights of our married life.' Wendel wiped the tears of laughter from his eyes. 'We danced until dawn. Sorry, Angel, but talking of dawn, I've kept you up far too late, haven't I?'

'Not at all,' Bethany protested, casting a surreptitious glance at the clock.

'Off you go to bed,' Wendel insisted. 'I'll clear up.'

Surveying the room this morning, it transpired that Wendel's idea of clearing up was to leave their dirty plates and cups on the draining board. Bethany squirted washing-up liquid into the bowl and set to with the scrubbing brush. Today was the start of her new job. Speaking of which, she thought, where was everybody?

A watery sunlight was trying to get on with the day, but the icy conditions outside proved too much for its weak stamina. Bethany shivered. She hoped the cast had invested in thermals to wear under their thin costumes. Water-bridge Manor didn't possess the most efficient heating system in the world.

The hands on the clock crept past the hour. Not only was there no sign of a film crew, but there was no sign of Wendel either. Bethany was beginning to wonder if the whole of yesterday's events had been nothing more than a bad dream. Bouncer pattered across the floor and stood beside her as she stared out of the kitchen window.

'I suppose you'd better go outside.' Bethany looked down at the dog. Neither she nor Bouncer viewed the prospect with much enthusiasm, but Bethany knew when to be firm. She wedged open the back door. A blast of cold air hit her in the face. Bouncer tried a tentative growl as a protest, but eventually, giving in with dignity, scuttled outside.

'Five minutes,' Bethany called after him before going in search of her rabbit.

Opening his cage, she let him out. 'Keep the noise down,' she warned. 'Wendel's asleep. And careful how you go. We don't want you tripping over anything.'

Furry bounded onto the living room carpet and began to explore his new surroundings. Bethany wondered if Catriona Cleeve was allergic to Giant Papillons. Furry loved nothing more than meeting people. Being shut up all day would probably stress him. A noise drew Bethany's attention to the kitchen.

'Morning, Angel,' Wendel called through.

'Have you seen the time?'

'Sorry, I overslept.'

'I meant, what happened to half past seven?'

'I presume it came and went.' Wendel spread marmalade on his toast and took a healthy bite.

'Sam Richards? Film crew? *Love Will Find a Way*?'

A guilty look crept over Wendel's face. He dropped his slice of toast back onto the plate. 'I meant to leave you a note,' he confessed. 'Sorry, I forgot.'

'Forgot what?' Bethany asked through clenched teeth.

'Ops have been suspended for the day. Something to do with the weather, I think — or was it equipment not arriving? I was only half-awake when I took the call.'

'So where is everyone?'

'Haven't a clue.'

There was a loud thud at the door. Wendel leapt to his feet. 'Is that Bouncer? I'll let him in.'

Bouncer shot into the kitchen and headed straight for the warmth of his basket, casting a baleful look in Bethany's direction. She ignored him. 'Filming's been suspended?' she asked in an attempt to clarify the situation.

'That's right, so I suggest you keep your head down and have a quiet day in. It might be the only chance you get, and you deserve it after clearing up all the mess in the garden.'

'It wasn't me,' Bethany pointed out.

Wendel was struggling to open a new

jar of marmalade and didn't immediately reply. Bethany took a better look out the window. All the evidence of yesterday's party had gone.

'Then it must've been the fairies.' Wendel sounded supremely unconcerned.

'I'm ringing The Goose and Galleon,' Bethany announced, 'to find out what's going on.'

'If you want me,' Wendel said as he scooped up his plate of toast, 'I'll be catching up with the news.'

'He's not taking calls from the public,' Bethany was told by whoever it was who answered her call.

'I'm not the public and he'll take this one, otherwise filming at Waterbridge Manor is cancelled.' Bethany adopted the tone she had often used in the past when faced with self-important officials. She was put through immediately. 'Sam?' she said.

'Glad to hear we're on first-name terms, Bethany,' Sam greeted her. 'What can I do for you?'

'You can tell me why you didn't bother to update me on today's schedule, for a start.'

'Didn't Wendel tell you?'

'Not until gone eight this morning.'

'I'm sorry.' Sam sounded genuinely regretful. 'We can't get the vehicles up the hill, so we thought we'd have an in-house read-through. Why don't you join us?'

'I've plenty to do up here.'

'Such as?'

Sam's question put her on the spot. 'Tidying up?' Bethany crossed her fingers. 'The garden's a mess.'

'I filled three bin liners,' Sam protested, 'and I scattered the ashes from the barbecue on the rose bed.'

'It was you?' Bethany gasped, unable to imagine their director doing the rounds with a black bin liner.

'Half past five this morning, and was it cold. I would have knocked on your door for a coffee but I didn't think you'd appreciate a social call that early in the day.'

'Thank you,' Bethany mumbled, embarrassed at having been caught out telling a fib.

'Don't mention it. It was our mess. Tell you what,' he suggested, 'why don't I come up to you? There are one or two things we need to discuss.'

Bethany began to feel uneasy at the thought of seeing him again. She couldn't put her finger on it, but there was something unsettling about Sam Richards. She was reminded of one of her grandmother's sayings: he was a square peg in a round hole. Romantic costume dramas were not Sam's thing, so what was he doing directing one?

'The news is nothing but high-powered conferences and financial stuff,' Wendel grumbled, turning off the television after Bethany had tracked him down in the library.

'Sam Richards is going to pay us a visit.' Bethany plumped up the cushions.

'That'll be nice.'

'Do you know anything about him?'

Bethany asked, settling down on the lumpy sofa Wendel occasionally used for his afternoon snooze.

'What do you want to know?'

'How did you meet him?'

'I'm not sure, really. I got a telephone call from an agent and he asked if I was interested in a filming project. Someone had mentioned to him that Waterbridge Manor was a suitable location. Before I knew it, contracts were signed, and you know the rest.'

'And Sam Richards?'

'I don't know what to make of him,' Wendel hedged.

'He was the one who cleared the litter from the garden at half past five this morning.'

'Was he now?' Wendel looked impressed.

They lapsed into silence. Bethany watched the coal fire flames create images in the grate. Lighting the fire was the one chore Wendel always undertook, and Bethany was pleased it was a tradition that hadn't lapsed. A sharp rap on the front door broke the silence.

'That'll be Sam.' Bethany struggled to her feet. 'I'll let him in.'

'Hey you, come back,' Wendel roared. 'Stop him!' he yelled as Bethany unlocked the main door.

'Quick,' she said as she pulled Sam inside and slammed the door behind him.

'I didn't expect quite such an enthusiastic greeting.' Sam dusted snow off his donkey jacket and took off his boots.

'It's my rabbit. Can you see him anywhere?'

'On the run, is he? Can't say I blame him. I'd do a runner if I could, only I'm the director and it's not allowed.'

'Got him,' Wendel bellowed from the lounge. 'Not before time, too. He was about to nibble a stray wire. Hang on while I return him to his hutch.'

He announced a few moments later, 'All clear. You can come in now. Morning, Sam.' The two men shook hands. 'If the two of you want to talk privately, I'll have a go at making coffee. Don't look so alarmed, Angel. It's a skill I've recently acquired, and if I say so myself it's not half bad. There's a Victoria sponge cake about the place too somewhere. I'll see if I can find it.'

'I'm sorry about the misunderstanding earlier,' Sam apologised. 'I should've spoken to you personally, but Wendel said you were asleep.'

'Do you ever get any sleep?' Bethany asked.

'It's a commodity in short supply when I'm filming,' Sam admitted.

'We're in here.' Bethany led him through to the library.

Sam sat beside her on her lumpy sofa and stretched out his socked feet in front of the fire. 'I've brought you a copy of the script.' He produced a bundle from his backpack. 'I thought you might like to know what the production is all about.'

'Isn't *Love Will Find a Way* a departure from your usual line of work?' Bethany felt compelled to ask.

'Do you know much about my previous films?'

'I saw *Dangerous Chance* recently.'

'I didn't know they were still showing that one.'

'It was two in the morning,' Bethany admitted.

'The graveyard slot.' Sam made a rueful face. 'In answer to your question, I decided to take a sabbatical to catch up with the things that matter in life. I travelled around, did some charity work, that sort of thing. Eventually I came home to find I'd been given another chance in the industry.'

'And the chance was *Love Will Find a Way?*' Bethany wasn't sure Sam's glib explanation ran entirely true. There were large gaps in his story, and she couldn't shake off the suspicion there was something he wasn't telling her.

'It's actually a very good script. Anthony Granger and Catriona Cleeve play the leads. It's Catriona's first starring role. She's had minor parts in one or two promising movies and her last role got good reviews. I think she's got a great future ahead of her.

Anthony's looking to develop his career too, and this film could be the vehicle to do it for him.'

'All the same, it's a departure from your usual type of thing.'

'Yes, it is, isn't it?'

Bethany had to content herself with the realisation that that was the only explanation she was going to get, so she changed the subject. 'You still haven't explained what my official duties are.'

'You must know Waterbridge Manor like the back of your hand.'

'I spent much of my childhood here.'

'Do you think you'll be able to deal with any ongoing emergencies? Keep people off my back?'

'I can try.'

'Good. Is there anything else before we have a read-through?'

'I still have your mobile phone.'

'Keep it. I've got several. I give out different numbers to different people, so you needn't worry that you'll upset anyone. The really important people make me ring them.'

Wendel appeared in the doorway. 'Coffee's ready. Can you take the tray? Someone's hammering on the door.'

'That'll be Lisolette — she plays Anthony's mother,' Sam explained to Bethany. 'We wanted a character actress for the part and Miss St James was available. She arrived in Steeple Maltravers this morning.'

'Lisolette St James?' Wendel looked frozen to the spot.

'Don't tell me you're a fan,' Bethany teased him.

The hammering on the door increased in volume. 'You look after Bouncer.' Sam thrust the dog in Bethany's direction. 'I'll get the door.'

Bethany shook his shoulder. 'Wendel, what's the matter?'

'Lottie Cronk,' he said in a voice a little above a whisper.

'Who's Lottie Cronk?'

'Lisolette St James.'

'What?'

'I went to school with her.'

'She's an old friend?' Bethany was

struggling to understand why the mention of her name was having such an effect on Wendel.

'She was more than that. I asked her to marry me.'

'You did what?' Bethany's raised voice set Bouncer barking again.

'Then I met Mary, and . . . ' Wendel ran out of words.

'And you stood me up.' The voice that had set thousands of male hearts fluttering interrupted them. Standing in the doorway of the library was one of the most ravishingly beautiful women Bethany had ever seen in her life.

4

'Silence, everyone. This is a take.'

Looking incredibly dashing in Regency costume and white breeches, Anthony Granger prepared to play out the challenging scene with his mother.

'Cheri, where have you been?' She pouted.

'Talking to Elena,' was Anthony's crisp reply.

'Such a charming infant,' Lisolette, playing the Dowager Duchess, cooed in a seductive French accent, 'and I love her to bits.'

'Then you're on my side.' Anthony was all eager young swain.

'These things, they have to be handled delicately.' Lisolette shrugged. 'Elena is the fourth daughter of an impoverished father.'

'Sir Henry Wick-Stanley's line is descended from William the Conqueror.'

'Whereas you, my darling, are the second son of an earl.' The Duchess narrowed her eyes.

'Exactly. Harry is the eldest son. He inherited the title, which means I am free to marry whoever I want to.'

'Which means,' the Duchess insisted, 'you must make an advantageous marriage.'

'You want me to marry a rich heiress, someone I do not have feelings for.'

Bethany was enthralled. The camera loved both Anthony and Lisolette. The chemistry between their two strong-willed characters threatened to set the drawing room on fire. Lisolette was wearing an auburn wig that emphasised the intensity of her green eyes, a perfect foil to Anthony's brooding matinee-idol sensuality.

'Cut,' Sam called as Anthony stormed out of the room. A loud crash followed his departure.

'I hope he hasn't broken his leg,' Johnny quipped.

Lisolette sauntered out of camera

shot. 'I think you'll find the culprit is closer to home.' She looked down at a guilty Bouncer standing in the middle of the remains of what had been a water-lily vase.

'Who let that dog in?' Sam bellowed.

'He slipped through when Anthony opened the door.' Lisolette cast Bethany a sympathetic look and mouthed the words *bad luck*.

'You know the rules. No animals allowed on set, and that goes for that wretched rabbit too.' Sam's eyes swung in Bethany's direction. 'I caught him trying to nibble one of our emergency cables.'

'Ease up, Sam,' Johnny chipped in. 'These things happen.'

Sam looked in no mood to compromise. 'See to it, Bethany and get that mess cleared up.'

'Give Bouncer to me.' Lisolette held out her arms to Bethany, who was now cradling the trembling animal. 'I'll hold him.'

'Not in that costume you won't, Miss

St James.' The wardrobe mistress leapt forward and draped a cloak around her shoulders.

The floor manager clapped his hands. 'Take five, everyone.'

'What did I miss?' Anthony, who had slipped back into the room, sidled up to Bethany. Bouncer licked his hand. Anthony eyed the scene of the disaster. 'Was this your fault?'

''Fraid so,' Bethany answered for Bouncer.

'And Sam's blaming you?'

'I wouldn't put it quite like that, but Wendel promised to keep an eye on him.'

'How about we chill out together? Fancy a coffee?' Anthony stifled a yawn. 'I hate early-morning shoots. By ten o'clock you're ready for lunch.'

The continuity assistant consulted her clipboard. 'Your hair needs seeing to. You're in the next shot. And you can't change your waistcoat. Everything has to look exactly the same.'

'Sorry, we'll have to put coffee on

hold.' Anthony waved at Bethany as a make-up assistant hustled him away.

Bethany finally tracked Wendel down in the library. 'Bouncer smashed a vase and almost ruined a take. Sit,' she ordered the terrier. Bouncer immediately slunk down in front of the fire.

'Sorry, Angel,' Wendel apologised. 'I got engrossed in other things.'

Bethany took a deep breath and prepared to contradict him. 'No you didn't.'

'What?'

'I want the truth, Wendel.' Bethany crossed her arms and waited.

'It's Lottie,' Wendel confessed.

'Lisolette St James? What about her?'

'I'm staying out of her way.'

'Why?'

Wendel screwed up his face. 'It's difficult to explain.'

'Is this anything to do with your past?'

'Sort of. Lottie's fond of making scenes. It's part of her artistic temperament, I suppose.'

'I'm sure Lottie's professional enough not to make a scene in front of everyone on set.'

'You don't know her.'

'Maybe not as well as you,' Bethany conceded, 'but your relationship with her was years ago.'

'She was a red-haired temptress in her day.' A dreamy look came into Wendel's eyes. 'All the men were in love with her.'

'Including you.'

'That was before I met Mary.'

Bethany knew the only way to treat Wendel was to be firm with him. 'Personal issues aside, filming here was your idea. You can't abandon your responsibilities.'

A gentle tap on the door interrupted them. Wendel made a gesture with his hands. 'Whoever it is, get rid of them.'

Bethany opened the door a fraction and peered round.

A make-up assistant was hovering outside. 'Sorry to interrupt you.'

'I'll be right out,' Bethany promised.

'It's actually Wendel we need.'

'Can't a man have any peace?' Wendel protested.

'Miss St James wants to see him.'

'Tell her I'm busy.'

'This is ridiculous.' Bethany was fast losing patience with her godfather. 'Wasn't it you who lectured me on the importance of not holding up filming? Something to do with budgets?'

'That was different,' was Wendel's truculent reply.

'Tell Miss St James that Wendel will be out shortly.' The make-up girl scuttled off in relief. 'Now what's all this really about?' Bethany turned back to face Wendel. 'What went on between the two of you yesterday?'

After the shock of Wendel being reconciled with his old flame, Sam and Bethany had made themselves scarce. The beginnings of a mild thaw had set in, and together they had slithered down the hill to The Goose and Galleon, where they spent the rest of the day working on the script with the cast. Bethany stood in for Catriona Cleeve, whose flight from America had been delayed due to the weather. Sam had proved good company; and when Anthony was called away to take a telephone call, he had assumed Anthony's role, playing it with such intensity that Bethany found she was blushing. Fortunately, most of the cast were engrossed in reading their own parts and didn't notice her discomfort as she and Sam read through the love scenes. She knew he was only acting a part, but she wished he wouldn't look as if he meant every word he was saying. She wanted to open a window but it had begun snowing again, forcing Sam to call an early halt to the proceedings to enable those not staying at The Goose and Galleon to make their way to their lodgings in safety.

He then insisted on escorting Bethany back up Maltravers Hill. His muscles strained against hers as they tackled the steep gradient. 'I'm not as fit as I used to be,' he panted. 'My legs may never speak to me again. How are you doing?'

'It's colder here than in Canada,' Bethany puffed in reply.

'What were you doing over there?'

'Amongst other things, visiting my mother. She lives in Toronto.' An image of Harland Somerville flashed into her mind. Bethany had not been running away, but Sam might not see it like that.

'I thought Wendel said you were nursing.'

'It was a temporary position. Here we are,' she said in relief, 'journey's end. Thanks for the escort.'

Sam refused her offer of a hot drink and Bethany watched him start the long trudge back down the hill. When he was no more than a blur in the distance, she went in search of Wendel, but a note on the kitchen table said he didn't want to be disturbed. There had been no sign of Lottie, and over a hurried breakfast that morning Bethany had thought it wiser not to ask, but things could not continue in the same vein.

'Nothing went on between us,'

Wendel had snapped.

'Then why are you scared to face up to her?'

'I'm not.'

'The truth, Wendel,' Bethany insisted.

'Seeing her again felt disloyal to Mary,' he confessed in a rush.

'Why?'

'I don't know. Lottie belongs to the past. Somehow the relationship doesn't feel right now.'

'No one's suggesting you rekindle your romance,' Bethany said, softening her voice.

'That's the trouble.' Wendel now looked thoroughly miserable.

'What is?'

'I think Lottie feels that now I'm single, perhaps we could be friends again.'

'Isn't that a good idea?'

'I'm not sure.'

'How do you feel about her?'

Wendel broke into a wistful smile. 'She reminds me of my youth. We had a lot of fun together. Have you any idea why she wants to see me?'

'None at all. But come on, we can't hang around all day.'

Another loud knock caused the door to vibrate. 'What's going on in there?' Bouncer whined at the sound of Sam's voice and hid his head under his front paws.

'Wendel will be out as soon as he's ready,' Bethany responded.

'Tell him to hurry up.'

'Five minutes to get yourself together,' Bethany ordered Wendel before sidling out of the library. 'And if you're not out in that time, I'm sending Sam in to get you.'

The director was pacing in the hall-way. Another of his mobile phones began to ring. He thrust it into Bethany's hands. She switched it to voice mail. 'Have you no control over your godfather?' he demanded.

Bethany bit down the retort hovering on her lips. Instead she asked, 'Why does Miss St James want to see Wendel?'

'All actors have fragile egos.' Sam was

still pacing the floor as he spoke. 'And with Catriona Cleeve due to start filming later in the week, Miss St James is probably feeling her years.'

'But she's a fantastic actress.'

'It seems she needs Wendel to bolster her ego.' Sam ran a hand through his increasingly dishevelled hair. 'See what you can do,' he pleaded.

While they had been talking, Wendel had opened the door. 'No need to trouble yourself further, Sam. I'll come.'

'Thank goodness that's settled.' Sam stomped off.

'For heaven's sake,' Bethany chided Wendel as he smoothed down his hair and straightened the collar of his casual shirt, 'most men would kill to be in your shoes. You look as though you're on your way to the guillotine in a tumbrel.'

'Miss St James is in the conservatory,' the make-up assistant informed them.

Anthony, with his hair freshly styled,

was now seated on the sofa. He patted the spare seat next to him. 'Hanging around like this never gets any easier.' He began to fidget as Bethany sat down. 'I suppose you don't feel like building a snowman?'

'You suppose right.' Bethany smiled, sympathising with his predicament.

'I'm not even allowed a coffee in case I spill it over this wretched waistcoat,' Anthony grumbled.

'How about a game of draughts?' Bethany suggested. 'I'm sure there's a board around somewhere.'

Twenty minutes later there was a commotion at the far end of the room. Lisolette St James appeared, all smiles, until she caught sight of Bethany. 'Take it off.' She pointed at Bethany's blouse.

Draughts scattered in all directions as Bethany jerked to her feet.

'It's unlucky to wear green on set.'

'Change it,' Sam snapped, 'before one of us has a nervous breakdown.'

'See what I mean?' Wendel gloated, standing to one side and tapping the side of his forehead. 'Difficult.' He didn't move his lips as he spoke. 'If you'll excuse me,' he now addressed Sam, 'I have a dog to take for a walk. I may be some time.'

★ ★ ★

That evening Bethany shook her head at the computer screen. 'It is unbelievable, Mum. In the background she could see her stepfather watching an ice hockey game.

'The Sprinters have scored!' he yelled. 'Hi, Bethany.' He blew her a kiss, 'Catch up with you later, sweetheart.'

'Run that past me again,' Zoe insisted when Ken had returned his attention back to the television.

'Have you ever heard of Lisolette St James?'

'I can't say I have, but I *have* heard of Sam Richards. Something to do with charity work? Feminist issues?'

'That doesn't sound like the Sam Richards I know.'

'I've probably got my wires crossed. How's Wendel?'

'He's gone mad.'

'Darling, isn't that a little harsh?'

'Is it the act of a sane individual to hold a garden party in the snow, then go and let your house out to a film crew without telling anyone?'

'He didn't *have* to tell anyone, did he?'

'Whose side are you on?' Bethany demanded.

'I'm not taking sides, darling, but you know Wendel. He's never done things by halves.'

'This time he's surpassed himself.'

'He was a bit of a boulevardier in his youth,' Zoe reminisced.

'Well he's reverting to type. Let me tell you, life at Waterbridge Manor is not easy.'

'It sounds like fun to me. So who's this Lisolette St James you mentioned?'

'She's an actress who happens to be a part of Wendel's past.'

'Sounds interesting.'

'He's making life impossible for the rest of us.'

'From what you say, it sounds as though Wendel's trying to move on. I mean, no one's suggesting he wasn't devoted to Mary, but she wouldn't have wanted him to mourn forever.'

Bethany looked at her mother in exasperation. 'Why couldn't he have taken up bridge? Or golf?'

'You know Wendel's never been one for joining things. Anyway, what's Anthony Granger like? Ken and I saw him in that sci-fi drama. It wasn't really my thing but it got rave reviews.'

'He's the only sane one of the bunch.'

'And?' Zoe prompted. 'You hesitated.'

'He's asked me out for a drink one evening,' Bethany admitted.

'Has he indeed? Are you going to accept?'

'Maybe, when the snow's melted. Most of the local roads are still snowbound.'

'You don't know what snow's all about,' Ken called over.

'Hello there,' Wendel said as he barged into the room. 'I thought I heard voices. Budge up, Angel, and let me talk to my second favourite girl.'

'Wendel, what's this I'm hearing about you and your old girlfriend painting the town red?'

Bethany left them to it. Out on the landing she paused. Now that everyone had gone home, it should be safe to let Furry have the run of the place.

Down in the conservatory, Bethany discovered the door to his hutch swinging open. There was no sign of the rabbit.

5

Merrill Sims gave Bethany a cheerful wave before parking the wardrobe van on the grass verge and jumping out of the cab. 'It'll be bliss to work from my own base,' she announced. 'I haven't been able to drive up the hill until today. I've a big favour to ask. Could I use a spare bedroom as storage space? These old costumes get crushed if I can't lay them out straight. It's a nightmare keeping them crease-free. What's wrong?' she asked, taking in Bethany's stricken face.

'Furry disappeared last night and I can't find him.'

'He wouldn't have gone far in the snow, would he?'

'He doesn't like the cold but he does love to explore.'

'Sam won't be best pleased,' Merrill said with a grimace. 'You know the rules. No animals allowed on set. Health and safety.'

'Furry hasn't found his way on set so far.'

'But if he did, and there was an incident . . . ' Merrill shrugged. 'You get my drift?'

Bethany nodded, casting a desperate look around the garden. Merrill glanced over her shoulder. 'Johnny was trying to organise transport up Maltravers Hill. Everyone's getting fed up with the walk. Shoes are being ruined now the snow is turning to slush.'

'How long have I got?' Bethany asked.

'Half an hour. Where do we start?'

'Upstairs is out of bounds.'

'Bounds, rabbit, good one,' Merrill joked. 'Sorry, I'm not helping matters am I? Shall I try the garden?'

'Wendel searched outside last night until the battery in his torch gave out.'

Merrill locked up the back of her van. 'Insurance,' she explained. 'Some of the costumes are valuable.' She pocketed the key. 'You do another trawl of the garden and I'll check downstairs. Back here in ten minutes?'

'Any luck?' Bethany pounced on Merrill as she reappeared around the side of the house.

'Not a sign of him. You?'

Bethany shook her head.

'He's such a sociable animal. He wouldn't recognise a threat,' she said.

Neither of them dared mention the word *fox*.

'We're running out of time.' Merrill glanced at her watch. 'I've got to get today's costumes ready.' She unlocked the back door of the van.

'Thanks for your help,' Bethany began, but her words were cut off by Merrill's loud shriek.

'Quick!' she yelled. 'Furry!'

Out of the corner of her eye, Bethany caught a streak of fur darting out of Merrill's van.

'He went that way. Get after him!' Merrill urged as the crew minibus hooted its horn.

'Good morning.' Wendel was in the kitchen sipping coffee when Bethany raced in.

'Furry . . . ' She fought to catch her breath. 'Did he come this way?'

'Didn't see him,' he replied with a distracted air. 'While you're here, Angel, there's something I have to tell you.'

'Not now.'

'It's about me and Lottie.'

'Later,' Bethany pleaded with him.

Wendel glanced to Bethany's right. 'Morning, Sam,' he delivered in hearty greeting.

Bethany's eyes were drawn to a dragonhead badge pinned to the lapel of the director's jacket. 'Where's Bouncer?' he asked.

'I'm about to take him for a walk.' Wendel nudged his basket. 'Stir yourself, lazybones.'

'Catriona Cleeve has arrived.' Sam's voice was brisk and businesslike. 'I don't need to remind everyone she has animal issues?'

'I'll leave Bouncer at The Goose and

Galleon after we've had our walk. The landlord won't mind.' Wendel clipped Bouncer's lead onto his collar.

'I'd better check on the day's schedule,' Bethany said, anxious to get away from Sam and carry on looking for Furry. She bit down her irritation as she heard Anthony calling her name.

'Go and see what he wants,' Sam said, 'and remember what I said about Catriona Cleeve's allergy. No dog hairs. And make sure Anthony's on hand to greet her when she arrives.'

'Hello, what's up?' Anthony asked as he kissed Bethany on the cheek. 'You're looking hot and bothered.'

'Can you keep a secret?'

'Probably not.' He grinned. 'But give me a try.'

'Furry's gone walkabout.'

'I thought Merrill looked odd crouched down on all fours down by the log basket.'

'This is serious.'

'You're right,' Anthony agreed. 'You couldn't have picked a worse time. Did you know Catriona Cleeve has a clause in her contract about her allergy to animal fur? Course you did. Silly question. Want me to help look for him?'

'Shouldn't you be in wardrobe?'

'Sam said you had to humour me.'

'I don't think searching for a runaway rabbit was what he had in mind.'

'Keep your voice down.' Anthony glanced over his shoulder. 'Suits of armour have ears around here. I think we'd better move on,' he added as a muffled curse in the background was followed by a dull thud.

Merrill accosted them in the hall. 'I've put the word round, so we're all on lookout.'

A grim-faced Sam strode towards them. 'Change of plan,' he announced. 'We'll do some stills in the morning room. Anthony, you're first. Bethany, can you see to Jim? He's cut his arm.'

'Sorry,' the technician apologised, 'the lamp fell over. It's only a surface cut but it won't stop bleeding.'

'Leave me to deal with this, Bethany,' Merrill offered, clutching the first-aid box. 'Do another quick tour of the garden; but if you see Catriona Cleeve, make yourself scarce.'

'I owe you one, Merrill.'

'Don't mention it.'

'Turn your head, Anthony,' Bethany heard Sam's voice coming from the morning room, 'and look in the direction of the window. Try not to blink.'

She hovered by the door, waiting for the right moment to slip past unnoticed. She could see Anthony resting a hand on the Georgian fireplace as he shifted position. His eyes caught hers, and with the faintest of winks he acknowledged her presence before slowly moving his head. Holding her breath, Bethany tiptoed across the polished floor. Her jaw ached with tension. If Sam should turn round, there was nowhere to hide.

Jim barged up to her, clutching his bandaged arm 'All done, Bethany.'

She sagged against the wall. Her cover was blown.

'Jim?' Sam called out. 'In here. I need Bethany too.'

With a sinking heart, she followed Jim into the morning room. A flurry of snow drifted past the window and the sky darkened. A collective groan went round the room. Bethany's heart sank. Furry would not survive another session out in the cold.

'Catriona Cleeve isn't going to like this,' Johnny Morton murmured. 'She's been used to California sunshine.'

'Quiet, everyone. Ready, Anthony?' Sam thrust his paperwork and stopwatch at Bethany. 'Write down any readings I give you.'

Anthony began turning his head again. Johnny Morton broke into a broad grin as a pair of rabbit ears appeared behind Anthony's head. A porcelain figurine moved gently along the mantelpiece. Anthony jerked as rabbit whiskers tickled the back of his neck. 'Hey, stop that.'

The quivering rabbit leapt down off the mantelpiece straight into Sam's arms, where it began to make snuffly noises and nestle into his neck.

'Don't they look sweet?' Merrill cooed. 'How about a selfie?'

'Don't you dare,' Sam threatened.

Bethany's eyes met Sam's over the tip of Furry's ears. 'He escaped last night,' she confessed. 'Wendel and I searched everywhere.'

Sam continued to tickle the rabbit behind his left ear. Bethany held out her hands. 'I'll take him.'

Sam shook his head. 'I thought you said the hutch was secure.'

'It was. It is,' Bethany insisted.

'It doesn't look like it to me. Don't you realise — ' His expression darkened but he got no further.

'Hate to interrupt,' Anthony broke in, 'but a car's driven up outside. Catriona Cleeve and . . . ' He peered out the window. ' . . . one other.'

'What's he doing here?' Sam muttered.

'You know him?' Anthony enquired.

'It's Harland Somerville.'

'Did you say Harland Somerville?' Bethany asked in a faint voice.

'Who's he?' Anthony wanted to know.

'Harland is the nephew of Leo Somerville,' Sam explained in an expressionless voice. 'His uncle is head of a consortium providing the capital finance for *Love Will Find a Way*.'

'You don't say. Come on, gang. Let's hear it for Catriona Cleeve.'

Everyone began to troop outside. Sam thrust Furry into Bethany's arms. 'No more great escapes — I mean it,' he warned before making his way outside to join the welcoming party.

Bethany stood rooted to the spot. The last time she had seen Harland Somerville had been the day his uncle, Leo Somerville, had fired her for irregular practices.

6

Bethany had forgotten how Harland's aftershave always gave her a headache. She kept a firm hand on the wire mesh of Furry's hutch and tried not to inhale too deeply.

'Sam Richards wouldn't want you anywhere near his production if he knew you were implicated in a fraud.'

Bethany could tell Harland was enjoying himself from the way his smile didn't reach his eyes. His expression always reminded her of a cat tormenting a mouse.

'He can hardly evict me from my godfather's house,' Bethany retaliated. 'And if you're trying to blackmail me, it won't work. I have nothing to hide.'

'No one believed you the last time you protested your innocence.' Harland's confident smile lingered on his lips. This was the sort of game he enjoyed playing.

'That's because I was up against your uncle.'

'Whereas this time you're up against a film schedule, one that's being financed by my uncle.'

Bethany could feel rabbit whiskers tickling her fingertips, a gesture that gave her comfort. 'What do you want from me?' she demanded.

'Things were left unfinished between us.'

'The last time we met, it was made clear to me that our lives were no longer going in the same direction.'

'You walked out on me. I don't like that.'

'I didn't like the way you left me to take the rap for your questionable financial dealings.'

'We could've worked things out between us.'

'Your uncle didn't seem to be of the same opinion. According to him, I was lucky to escape prosecution.'

'It wouldn't have come to that. We

did nothing illegal.'

'I did nothing at all.'

'I've missed you, Bethany,' Harland changed tack. 'You always were full of spirit. Perhaps, now that the dust has settled, we can revive our acquaintance?'

Bethany's lip curled in distaste. The idea of having anything more to do with Harland Somerville was abhorrent to her. 'I have to get back to work.'

'We haven't finished.'

'I told you I have nothing to say to you. And as for reviving our relationship, you know my answer.'

'In that case, you leave me with no choice.' An ugly expression crossed Harland's face.

'What are you doing?'

Bethany tried to stop him but she was too late. With one slow movement, he flicked the latch on the rabbit hutch. The door swung open. Furry regarded Harland with an intense stare and to Bethany's relief decided to stay put.

'There you are.' Anthony Granger

breezed into the conservatory, where he took in the scene. 'Hello, I see the door's gone again. Have you been up to your old tricks?' He nudged the rabbit back inside and secured the latch. 'I'll get the chippy to do a repair job on the hutch if you like, Bethany. He's a wizard with wood, and I really can't have old Furry here upstaging my photo shoots. They might offer him the lead in my place.' His smile didn't waver. 'I don't believe we've been introduced.'

He turned his attention to Harland Somerville, and Bethany seized her moment to slip away. She ran upstairs to her room and doused her face in cold water, then dried it with a towel. She knew she ought to get away before Harland did some real damage to the production, but she couldn't leave without saying goodbye to Wendel, and he hadn't come back from his walk with Bouncer. She glanced out of the window and saw to her dismay that Harland's sleek sports car was blocking the drive. No one would be able to leave until he moved it.

Bethany sank onto the bed. Harland would take pleasure in jeopardising the filming. She knew there was no limit to the depths to which he would sink, but this time many more people would be involved if he stirred up trouble. Leo Somerville would probably withdraw his funding and the production would collapse. Of all the horrible coincidences, this had to be the worst.

But *was* this a coincidence? Bethany was struck by a ghastly thought. Was Harland stalking her? Had he found out that Wendel Nelson was her godfather? She had never introduced the two men to each other, but someone had suggested that Waterbridge Manor would be a good place to film.

Bethany straightened her shoulders. Cowering in her room was not her style. She had to find Sam.

'There you are.' He was waiting for her at the foot of the stairs. 'These are for you.' He held up a wad of paper.

'What are they?' Bethany asked.

'Your messages. Anthony found your mobile in the conservatory and gave it to me. It's been ringing nonstop.' Sam put on a pair of spectacles to read them. 'Johnny Morton's sister has found a mate for Furry. She thought a companion might prove a useful displacement activity and stop him mounting escape bids, so Johnny's gone to collect said companion. He'll be back later.' Sam's horn-rimmed glasses leant him the air of a college professor inspecting a student's work. 'Are you listening to me?' he demanded, peering over the top of them.

Bethany flushed. Her mind had been wandering. She had no right to be thinking that with a minor makeover Sam could be half-presentable. There were more important issues at stake.

'Wendel wants you to know he and Ms St James won't be back until later. They've gone off together somewhere.'

'Sam,' Bethany interrupted him, 'there's something important we have to talk about.'

'I haven't finished,' Sam insisted in a firm voice. 'Harland Somerville — ' Bethany's heart sank at the mention of his name. ' — says you're a fraudster who narrowly escaped a custodial sentence, and unless I want him to take things further with his uncle, I am to let you go immediately.' Sam removed his glasses. 'Now I'm done.'

The only sound to disturb the tranquillity of Waterbridge Manor was the gentle slide of snow melting off the roof.

'It's not how it sounds,' Bethany said in a hollow voice.

'I'm listening.'

'Harland and I worked together for his uncle Leo Somerville.'

'Go on.'

The expression on Sam's face made her want to shiver. 'I'll leave.' All the fight went out of Bethany. Harland was right — no one would believe her, so what was the point in trying to explain the situation? She had been beyond naïve in her dealings with him, and it embarrassed her to admit she had been so easily duped.

'Don't talk such nonsense.' Sam now sounded disgusted with her. 'This is your home.'

'It's Wendel's home and it's not non-sense. Harland has the power to bring the production crashing down around our ears.'

'How?'

'By telling his uncle about me.'

'Leo Somerville may be many things, but he isn't a fool. He's invested heavily in *Love Will Find a Way*, and there are zillions of clauses and contracts involved. Harland couldn't close us down even if he wanted to.'

'Leo's a powerful man.'

'He's also responsible to his investors. He has a lot riding on this one, and he wouldn't make an unwise commercial decision on the whim of his nephew.'

'Then what are we going to do?'

'As far as I'm concerned, it's business as usual.' Sam paused, then asked in a softer voice, 'Why didn't you come to me the moment you saw Harland with Catriona on his arm?'

'Because I was looking after Furry. I didn't want Catriona having an asthma attack.' It hurt Bethany's throat to swallow. 'I don't know how I got into this mess,' she admitted in a croaky voice.

'A question I've frequently asked myself on more than one occasion.' He looked pensive for a moment, then held out his hand. 'Do we have a deal?'

'To do what?'

'No running away?'

'You mean I've still got the job?'

'Your position here was never in doubt. I can't control this lot on my own and you seem to have the magic touch. Everyone listens to you. I'd probably have a walk-out on my hands if you were dismissed.' He gave her an enquiring look. 'What's it to be?'

'I'll stay on, if you're sure it won't cause a disruption.'

'I've never been more certain of anything in my life.'

'And my continued presence won't jeopardise filming?'

'No way.'

'In that case, deal,' agreed Bethany.

Sam's handshake was firm and the touch of his palm against hers reassuring. She noticed a pale band of flesh on his ring finger and wondered if the rumours of a marriage had been the reason for his unexplained disappearance.

'You know,' confided Sam, 'I think your friend Harland overestimates his own importance.'

Mention of her antagonist's name drew Bethany back to the present. 'He's not my friend, and where is he now?' she asked in a guarded voice.

'He's left for the day.'

'He didn't stay on to watch Catriona's debut?'

Sam made a gesture with his hands. 'Haven't you noticed how quiet everything is?'

Bethany had been so wrapped up in her own troubles that she hadn't realised there was none of the usual background chaos. 'Harland hasn't brought production to a halt?' she asked, still unable to believe Sam's assurance that Harland was not a force to be reckoned with.

'Nothing so dramatic. The snow got there first. It brought down a power line. We have no electricity, and according to the news we're unlikely to be reconnected for the rest of the day.'

'What about the generator?'

'It wouldn't be powerful enough for our needs. I'm afraid the crew are a superstitious lot, and after someone began telling spooky stories they all got a tad unsettled and decamped en masse to The Goose and Galleon, vowing never to return to Waterbridge Manor until power was restored.'

'I'm sorry.'

'What are you apologising for now?' Sam frowned.

'I don't know. Am I a jinx? I mean, everything's going wrong.'

'This is nothing. You should see some

of the shoots I've been on. This one's a walk in the park by comparison. Fancy a sticky bun?'

'Is that film-speak for another read-through?'

'No. Molly from catering has left us a plate of buns and the camping stove if we want to boil up some water. I think she was worried we might starve or die of thirst, and no one's allowed to do that on her watch. You make the tea and I'll sort out the buns.'

'Shouldn't you be down with the others in The Goose and Galleon?'

'They need their down time. They're a good bunch, and they'll work extra hard tomorrow if they think they've got away with kicking over the traces today. So — buns?'

The hurricane lamp cast shadows across the kitchen as Bethany and Sam prepared their snack.

'Did you decamp to Canada because of Harland?' Sam asked, spreading jam over one of the buns.

'Not entirely. My mother's married

to a man who works for one of the big power companies and I was overdue a visit. While I was there I got a temporary job as companion to an elderly lady.'

'And that's why Wendel sold me the story about you being a nurse?'

'I did start my training but I never finished it. My parents' marriage broke up and I went through a rebellious phase.'

The warmth of the tea began to spread through Bethany's chilled body. She didn't know why she was telling Sam her life history, but he was an easy person to talk to. 'This reminds me of the time when my mother and I stayed in Ken's log cabin in the mountains,' she confided. 'It was cosy but very back-to-nature.'

'Sometimes we need to take a step back in time,' Sam agreed.

'Is that what you did when you took time out?' Bethany asked, then shook her head, immediately regretting the question. 'I apologise. It's none of my business.'

Sam didn't speak for a few moments, then said, 'I took time out because — '

A loud crash outside had them both jumping to their feet. 'What was that?' Bethany could feel her heart thumping in her ears.

'I suppose you really don't have a resident ghost?' Sam cast an anxious look out of the window.

Lights flashed at the end of the drive. 'Not one carrying a torch and riding a motorbike.'

'I don't follow.' Sam frowned.

'It's Wendel, and I think he's demolished the garden gate.'

'Hello!' Her godfather waved at them from the end of the pathway as Bethany opened the back door, letting in a rush of raw air. 'Stay where you are. The temperature's dropped and it's like a skating rink out here. All the melted snow has refrozen. I couldn't stop the old girl in time,' he explained, slapping the bike's handlebars. 'Be with you in a moment when I've checked everything's OK here.'

'I'd better get some more tea on the go.' Bethany began to refill the saucepan and put it on the camping stove as they heard Wendel's boots clomping down the drive. He nudged open the door.

'I've never known weather like it in all the years I've lived here.' He began to unwind his scarf. 'My foot slipped on the pedals and I lost control. Sorry if I gave you both a shock. Is that tea and buns? I'm starving.'

'What have you done with Bouncer, and where's Lottie?' Bethany demanded.

'I didn't know you rode a motorbike,' Sam enthused.

'Feel free to borrow it any time you like,' Wendel replied. 'I keep it down in the village for emergencies.'

'You'll have to show it to me in the morning.'

Wendel's face lit up. 'The bike? I'd be delighted to, although it may need separating from a couple of fence panels. Never mind, worse things happen at sea. Bouncer's playing darts in The Goose and Galleon,' he said in reply to Bethany's question, 'and Lottie's caught the last train out of town.'

'She's done what?' Sam stopped smiling.

'That's what I came to tell you. She said to say she's had enough of the countryside, and she's gone back to civilisation until the snow clears.'

7

'Will someone please see to that dog?' Sam shouted.

'It's my fault.' Catriona looked as though she were about to burst into tears. Far from being the spoilt super-brat everyone had been expecting, she turned out to be a sweet girl for whom nothing was too much trouble.

'You can't help your allergy,' Merrill soothed her, then pulled a face. 'But something's going to have to be done about Bouncer. My, he's got a pair of lungs on him.'

'I could take him for a walk,' Bethany offered. 'That usually calms him down. He doesn't like being shut up inside.'

'Anything to stop that noise. By the way, where's the — ' Sam cast a wary glance in Catriona's direction. ' — r-a-b-b-i-t?' He spelt out the word carefully.

'I'll go find out.'

Anxious not to draw further attention to the situation Bethany, sidled out of the room. Further investigation in the kitchen revealed that Furry had managed to find his way into Bouncer's basket and fallen asleep. An outraged Bouncer was making his objection clear in no uncertain terms. 'Be quiet,' Bethany hissed. Bouncer froze mid-bark, a reproachful look in his eyes, before trying a tentative wag of his tail.

Johnny Morton struggled through the back door, carrying what appeared to be a large dog crate. 'Time for some action, I think, judging by the noise.' He deposited his load down on the kitchen table and brushed dirt off his hands. 'Jules is a French Lop.' From the other side of the wire mesh, two dark eyes inspected Bethany. 'According to my sister's expert knowledge on the subject, Papillons were a French breed, so the guys can chew over the old days together. What do you think?'

'I'll agree to anything if only to keep the peace.'

'It gets you like that after a while, doesn't it? Wait until you've been in the business as long as I have. So, where do you want me to put Jules?'

'If you wait while I fasten Bouncer's lead, you can go round the back to the conservatory. I'm taking him for a walk.'

'Wrap up well. It's arctic out there. My feet are freezing. How's everyone getting on with Catriona Cleeve?'

'I like her,' admitted Bethany as she struggled into the sturdiest pair of boots she could find and wrapped a woollen scarf around her neck.

'I've always had a bit of a crush on her.' Johnny gave a shamefaced smile.

'I wouldn't have thought her films were your sort of thing.'

'In the beginning I watched her early roles to learn about camera focus and all that other stuff, then I became hooked. The camera loves her. Did you ever see *Sweet Moment of Truth*? I predict it's going to be a classic.'

'I never took you for a romantic. But

I ought to warn you, you've got competition.'

'Harland Somerville?' Johnny wrinkled his nose.

'You know about him?'

'I've heard about him, none of it good. He's always threatening people with his uncle if he doesn't get his own way.'

'That about sums him up.'

'Can't waste time worrying about him. Some of us have to work for our living. Now, are you ready?' Johnny inspected Bethany's appearance. 'You seem to be wearing enough clothes for a polar expedition.'

Bouncer began tugging at his lead. 'Can you see to the rabbits?' Bethany asked. 'I don't know if I can hold him much longer.'

'Leave everything to me. You get outside in the fresh air. You're looking peaky, if you don't mind my saying so.'

'I'm fine,' Bethany assured Johnny. 'And I'm glad you're back.'

'Words to warm my heart. See you.'

Bethany's boots crunched over the fresh snow and her cheeks tingled in the sharp morning air. Bouncer strained at the leash, over-keen to explore the snow-laden sights and smells.

The Beacons were misted in clouds that promised further snowfall. Bethany's boots sank into deeper snow as they headed in the direction of Baker's Field, one of her favourite walks. A pheasant strutted across their path, its tawny chest striking a vivid contrast against the wintry landscape. Bethany ducked her head under a stray branch spiked with a crisp frost. She loved days like this.

As she strode along, she began to convince herself that Harland Somerville posed little threat. He had no authority over filming; and even if he went telling tales to his uncle, she hoped that what Sam said was true. Leo Somerville was first and foremost a businessman. Petty revenge wouldn't interest him unless it was to his benefit, and there would be no benefit in halting filming of *Love Will Find a Way*. All the same, it was the most horrible twist of fate to bump into Harland the moment her life was getting back on an even keel.

She bent down to unclip Bouncer's lead. 'Don't go far.' She raised a warning finger that the terrier proceeded to ignore. With a joyful bark, he bounded off in the direction of the trees. At some stage Bethany knew she would have to go after him, but right now she was content to take in the wild and beautiful scenery that had been Wendel's home for many years.

Bethany bit her lip, wondering what exactly was going on between her godfather and Lottie. She knew him well enough to realise when he was fudging the issue, and the story he'd spun about Lottie having had enough of the countryside and disappearing back to the bright lights didn't ring true. For her part, Lisolette St James was wise enough to recognise that walking off set was professional suicide.

The Dowager Duchess de Montchapelle was a plum role for an actress of her years. Competition for the part would have been fierce, and Lottie wasn't the sort of person to throw away the chance of a lifetime on a whim.

So what was she up to? And what had Wendel been trying to tell Bethany about Lottie in the kitchen when she had been looking for Furry? She began to wish she had paid more attention.

Bouncer's excited barking drew Bethany's thoughts back to the present. She trudged towards the source of the noise. A giggling little girl was throwing snowballs in the air and Bouncer was trying to catch them. Bethany laughed out loud at the sight of their antics, causing the child to drop her ammunition and run off in the direction of a crouched figure wearing an old-fashioned duffle coat.

'I hope my dog isn't being a nuisance,' she called over to the pair of them. 'He's very friendly and wouldn't hurt a soul.' Bouncer gave a supporting bark, his tail thwacking the side of Bethany's boots.

The crouched figure stood up. 'Would you care to join us?' he asked.

'Anthony?' Bethany moved slowly forward. 'What are you doing here?'

'Building a snowman.'

Bethany looked down at the child clutching his trouser leg.

'This is my daughter. Kiara, meet Bethany. She's one of the ladies I work with.'

'Hello.' Kiara gave a shy smile and moved in closer to her father.

'Your daughter?' Bethany didn't know what else to say.

'Why don't you and Bouncer make some more snowballs,' Anthony suggested to Kiara, 'while Bethany and I get the base of the snowman going?'

'I didn't know you had a daughter.' Bethany began patting some snow into place. 'I mean, it's absolutely none of my business of course.'

'Officially I'm not supposed to be married,' Anthony explained.

Bethany thumped the snow down hard with her hands. 'Is that why you carry on acting like you're single?' she couldn't resist asking.

'What?' Anthony frowned.

'Asking me out for a drink?'

'It's not like that.'

'It never is.'

'Perhaps if you'd let me explain . . . '

'Go on.'

'When I met Sally, she had no idea what I did for a living. That's what drew me to her in the first place. In this business it's very easy to get out of touch with what's normal. I think that's why so many relationships break down. Sally isn't impressed by all the glitz and hype, and I respect that. When we decided to get married, we chose a discreet country house hotel. All members of staff were made aware that if one word of the ceremony reached the ears of the press, then they were out of a job. My publicist knows, but he's chosen not to mention anything about it, and for public relations purposes he's kept up the pretence that I'm a bachelor.'

'Does Sam know?'

Anthony shook his head. 'Can I rely on you not to say anything?'

'You have my word,' Bethany promised.

They worked quietly on the snowman for a few moments, Bethany digesting all that Anthony had told her.

'Sally and I have a houseboat on the Thames, but we're going to have to move. It really isn't big enough with a growing family.' Anthony was breathing heavily from the effort of packing down the snow.

'Is Kiara your only child?'

'Sally's expecting our second child at the end of the month. Naturally she was concerned that I could be away filming at a crucial time, so it was decided she'd join me up here. I try to be with her every moment I can. With Lisolette St James disappearing overnight, my schedule's been put on hold, so I'm taking advantage of an unexpected break in filming, leaving Sam to concentrate on Catriona's scenes.' Anthony paused from patting down more snow. 'About our date . . . ' he began.

Bethany looked away. 'Please, don't. I've heard all the excuses.'

'Not this one, you haven't. I wanted to introduce you to Sally. She's been getting lonely with only Kiara for company, and I thought if you were agreeable to the idea we could look after Bouncer for you. Our cottage would make a convenient temporary home for him, especially now that Catriona's arrived. Furry's included in the invitation too. I wouldn't want him feeling left out.'

Bethany smiled at Anthony, awash with relief. She liked him, and the thought of him doing anything to distress his wife was too dire to contemplate.

'You're not doing very well,' a childish voice interrupted them. 'How come you've stopped working?'

'Sorry.' Anthony began moving more snow about the place. 'Honestly, there are times when my daughter is worse than Sam Richards. Get shovelling for goodness sake, otherwise we'll never hear the end of it.'

'Where's Sally now?' Bethany asked as she did Anthony's bidding.

'Having a rest. She's feeling tired, so I said I'd take Kiara for a walk. That's when we bumped into Bouncer. What's your reason for playing truant?'

'The usual. The animals have been misbehaving; and with Catriona's allergies, I thought it might be a good idea to give everyone some space.'

'Better,' Kiara trilled as a snowball landed at Bethany's feet.

Picking it up, Bethany lobbed it back, and soon a full-scale snowball fight was in progress. An accurate blow from Anthony knocked Bethany's bobble hat off her head. She responded with an equally accurate missile, and soon everyone was running around bare-headed and breathing hard with laughter as the fight gained momentum. No one noticed the flash from the trees as a crouching onlooker took shot after shot of the happy scene.

'Enough,' Anthony pleaded as another lucky snowball downed him. 'I'm too old for this sort of thing. Think of my insurance liability. Sam will never forgive me if I break a leg.'

Bouncer licked his face, and with scant regard for Anthony's starring role status began to bury him in more snow.

'Perhaps we'd better call it a day,' Bethany agreed, brushing snow off her jacket and re-clipping Bouncer's lead.

No one heard the sound of a car reversing slowly out of its hiding place and driving off down Maltravers Hill.

8

Harland Somerville strolled into the billiard room of The Goose and Galleon and peered over Sam's shoulder. 'She takes a good photo, I'll say that for Bethany.'

Sam swung round to confront him. 'It's Bethany?' He had been studying the photo, trying to work out the identity of the female rolling in the snow with Anthony Granger. The picture had gone viral on social media, causing renewed speculation about Sam's unexplained disappearance from the film world and his equally unexpected return. Chat rooms had been buzzing, stimulated by the news blackout on *Love Will Find a Way*. The picture of Anthony Granger, the star of the picture, was the first to hit the headlines and was receiving mega-publicity.

'Don't you recognise her?' Harland feigned surprise as Sam continued to frown at him. He studied the photo again.

'I tried to warn you about her, but you wouldn't listen.' Harland tapped Sam's screen with his finger. 'There's your proof. Bethany Burnett is trouble.'

'Trouble?'

'She's deliberately flouted the news blackout ruling.'

'I need to speak to Anthony,' Sam said, ignoring Harland's provocation.

'Good idea,' Harland agreed. 'But nobody appears to have seen him this morning. Perhaps he's with Bethany,' he suggested. 'She's good at running away.'

'Was there anything else?' Sam towered over Harland as he closed his laptop and stood up.

'Not really.' Harland picked up a billiard cue and leaned across the table to practise an experimental shot. 'Although I did promise to update my uncle on the situation here after I safely delivered Catriona Cleeve into your care, without I may add any press intrusion.' He played his shot before adding, 'I understand your other star, Ms St James, hasn't been seen on set for a couple of days.'

'She's been taking some time out,' Sam replied.

Harland chalked his cue. 'A word of advice, Sam. You're going to have to keep better tabs on your stars if you don't want stories circulating about unrest on set.'

'I trust I can rely on your discretion to stop any rumours of that nature?' Sam asked with an impatient frown.

'Naturally.' Harland's smile was as insincere as his voice. 'Although you need to remember that Catriona's schedule is very tight. My uncle wouldn't be pleased to hear you've been keeping her hanging around because Ms St James took it into her head to walk out.'

'Neither would he be pleased to hear you'd been causing unnecessary unrest amongst the crew.'

Harland pocketed his ball before turning his attention back to Sam. 'To change the subject, how are things going with The Dragon?' he enquired.

Sam swung back to face him. 'The Dragon?' he queried.

'I've been hearing things.' Harland looked less sure of himself.

'More stories?'

'It wasn't entirely coincidence that you chose to film at Waterbridge Manor, was it?'

'Wasn't it?'

'Goodness knows why, but my uncle seems to have a high opinion of Bethany.'

'So do I,' Sam said. 'But if you're worried about her status here, why don't you have a word with your uncle?'

'It doesn't do to get clever with me,' Harland threatened, an ugly flush staining the base of his neck.

'If you'll excuse me,' Sam spoke in a quiet voice.

'Don't let me keep you.' Harland's smile didn't reach his eyes. 'I know you've got a busy morning ahead of you.'

'Transport's out on a call, Sam,' George called through from the breakfast room. 'Wendel's motorbike is here. He won't mind you borrowing it so long as you don't land up in a ditch.' George grinned. 'It's in the outhouse.' He dangled the keys under Sam's nose. 'You look as though a change of air might do you good.'

Sam pocketed the keys. 'If you spot any reporters hanging around . . . ' he began.

'They'll get nothing out of me,' George promised.

Sam found Bethany and Wendel sharing coffee in the conservatory of Waterbridge Manor.

'How did it hold the hill?' Wendel nodded towards his bike. Sam had lodged it against the wall in the lean-to. 'Tracking's not off, is it? The garage said they'd fixed it, but you can never be too sure about these things. What about the tyre pressure?' He leaned forward anxiously. 'I haven't had a chance to test it yet. The roads have been too slippery.'

'Everything's fine,' Sam reassured him, his eyes fixed on Bethany.

'Good. You never know after you have an argument with a gate what sort of damage you're going to cause.'

Wendel's glance followed that of Sam's as he looked at the discarded newspaper on the coffee table. Both men registered their distaste.

'I don't have to tell you that none of this is our fault, do I?' The tone of Wendel's voice became less friendly. 'Neither do I expect to hear that Bethany's been made a scapegoat for infringing on your news blackout, something she knew nothing about.'

'Wendel,' Bethany cautioned, but Wendel wasn't listening.

'Bethany's reputation has suffered enough at the hands of Harland Somerville.'

'Unfortunately none of what happened on this occasion can be laid at Harland's door,' Sam pointed out.

Wendel was still having none of it. 'I'm not so sure. I wouldn't have put it past him to pay that snapper to stalk her.'

'That's a serious allegation, Wendel; one you would be wise not to repeat.'

'Which is why I'm only telling you about my suspicions. Anyway,' Wendel added, kissing Bethany's cheek, 'take my advice, Angel, and don't stand any nonsense from anyone.'

Bethany squeezed his hand and cast a look in Sam's direction. 'I can look after myself,' she said.

'That's my girl. I'll be off then. Bouncer needs exercise.' He nudged the snoozing dog with his foot. 'Sam, you'll be pleased to hear I don't have it in mind to play snowballs with anyone. We're going to take an old-fashioned walk through the woods, but if any photographer tries to take my picture they could be in for a shock. My boxing skills aren't so rusty that I can't remember how to hook a haymaker. Come on, Bouncer.'

The kitchen was over quiet after Wendel and Bouncer had left. Bethany looked down at the photo of her flat on her back in the snow with Anthony falling on top of her.

'I presume this photo's of you?' Sam asked.

'There's no point denying it, is there?'

'You haven't been officially identified.'

'It is me,' Bethany confirmed. 'I suppose Harland told you?' Sam nodded. 'I had no idea this sort of thing could happen.'

'It's a hazard of our profession. Maybe I should've warned you,' Sam acknowledged.

'I'm not making excuses for my behaviour, because I don't think I did anything wrong.'

'There's no limit to the length some of these photographers will go to get a scoop, and unfortunately you weren't on private property, so there's nothing we can do about it.'

'What happens now? I mean, it's not serious, is it?'

'The public relations agency believes there's no such thing as bad publicity and that we should make some mileage out of it.'

'What sort of mileage?' Bethany asked, a note of concern in her voice.

'They want to issue a statement to the effect that the female in the photo and Anthony are more than good friends.'

'They can't do that without my permission. Besides which, it's not true.'

'I'm of the opinion we should ignore it.'

Bethany felt a surge of hope. 'There are more important things going on in the world than a film star having a snowball fight,' she insisted.

'My feelings entirely. But there are certain sections of the press devoted to this type of thing.'

Bethany looked at the photo again. It was a stroke of luck that neither Kiara nor Bouncer featured in any of the photos. But when Sally, Anthony's wife, saw them, what was she going to think? Not only was Anthony married, but he was a father, and his wife was expecting their second child.

'Have you spoken to Anthony this morning?' she asked Sam.

'All his calls are being directed to voice mail.'

'Wendel's advice is to keep my head down.' Bethany could hardly bear to look at Sam.

'Do you always follow your godfather's advice?'

'Right now he's the only person I can trust.'

'You can trust me too,' Sam insisted. 'So if there's anything you want to tell me . . . ?'

'No.' Bethany shook her head. 'There's nothing.' She dreaded to think of the consequences if Sam found out that she knew about Anthony's marriage and hadn't told him. She really needed to speak to Anthony, but like Sam she had had no luck in contacting him.

'Any more of that coffee on the go?' Sam eyed up the percolator.

Bethany refilled her own mug and poured Sam a fresh one. Sam stirred his coffee thoughtfully. 'That message I took for you from Anthony — you had a date, didn't you?'

'Which we didn't keep because of the power cut, if you remember. And there is absolutely no truth in any of this nonsense.' Bethany pushed one of the more explicit tabloids away in disgust. 'I took Bouncer for a walk and bumped into him.'

'Whereupon you started throwing snowballs at each other?' Sam queried with a wry twist to his lips. 'As you do.'

'We began to build a snowman and things got out of hand.' Bethany knew she was making a bad job of explaining what had happened, and she could tell by the expression on Sam's face that he was having difficulty believing her.

'What was Anthony doing in Baker's Field?'

'You'll have to ask him.' Bethany had

run out of invented stories and hoped Anthony would be able to come up with something better.

'When did you last have anything to eat?' Sam asked.

'I don't remember.'

'Hungry?' She nodded. 'So am I. I missed out on breakfast.' He inspected a plate of abandoned cakes. 'I'm not sure how fresh they are. They're probably yesterday's leftovers.'

'Shouldn't you be directing something instead of drinking coffee and eating almond slices?' Bethany helped herself to one.

'Probably. But as Merrill's doing wardrobe fittings, and there's been a snag regarding Catriona's wig, and we can't shoot outside because there's snow on the ground, and Anthony isn't answering his mobile, and Lottie's gone walkabout, the answer to your question is no.'

'Did I hear someone taking my name in vain?' They both jumped at the sound of Lottie's voice. 'Almond slices?

Don't you dare snaffle them all, Sam.'
Lisolette St James paused in the doorway, wearing a bright orange trouser suit and looking every inch the star that she was.

'Where have you been?' Sam demanded.

'Did you miss me?' Lottie asked with a wicked smile. 'Bethany,' she said as she came forward and kissed her on both cheeks, 'what have you been up to in my absence? It is you in that photo, isn't it? I love a good scandal.' She sat down. 'Now, darlings, fill me in on all the gossip, and don't leave anything out.'

9

'I've had to cover for you with Sam and it hasn't been easy,' Bethany hissed to Anthony during a break in rehearsals.

'You didn't tell him about Sally?'

'Of course I didn't. I said I bumped into you and we had a snowball fight. I'm not sure he believed me, but I was thinking on my feet.'

'Thanks.' Anthony drew her to one side, away from prying eyes. 'I took the morning out to calm Sally down. Kiara's been going on about how much fun we had playing in the snow. She's always wanted a dog, but living on a houseboat it hasn't been possible. Sally's worried the press are going to find out about her, and what with one thing and another we're not having an easy time.'

'Would it help if I had a word with her?' Bethany volunteered.

Anthony fixed her with his hypnotic blue eyes. 'Best not rock the boat. She didn't have a good night's sleep, so she was going to rest up this afternoon.'

'Don't you think you ought to make a clean breast of things and tell Sam about Sally?'

'Difficult one.' Anthony grimaced.

'The longer you leave it, the worse it's going to get.'

'You don't have to tell me. I could strangle all paparazzi. Who would've thought someone would be so desperate to get a picture that they'd resort to hiding up a tree? What a way to earn a living.'

'Living or not, we're going to have to do something.'

'Such as?'

'Stopping the publicity department making something of our relationship might be a good place to start.'

'I may be able to offer a solution on that one.' Anthony adjusted the ruff of his Regency shirt.

'How?'

'Catriona's offered to help.'

Bethany looked across to where the young actress was in deep discussion with Lottie. 'How?'

'She's happy to stand in for you.'

Bethany switched her attention back to Anthony.

'Harland Somerville's been hanging around Catriona and making a nuisance of himself,' he explained. 'In an attempt to put him off, Catriona told him there's a significant other in her life. She thought if we pretended I was that person, it might do the trick.'

Catriona had finished talking to Lottie and now smiled nervously at Bethany. For all her beauty, Bethany couldn't help feeling sorry for the actress. She also felt that she ought to stand up for herself a bit more, but then who was she to criticise? Bethany hadn't made such a good job of things with Harland, and Catriona was offering a lifeline.

'What's Sally going to make of all this, and won't you be getting a reputation as a love rat?'

'That's the good part about it. Sally knows Catriona from way back.'

'I thought you said Sally wasn't in the entertainment business.'

'She wasn't, and neither was Catriona in the early days. The girls studied design together at college, but Catriona left after the first year to pursue her acting career.'

'Have you run this idea past Sam?' Bethany couldn't shake off the feeling that despite his outward show of support, Sam didn't totally trust her; and if Anthony's secret should come to light, then he would have every reason not to.

'I wanted to check that you were OK with the plan,' Anthony said. 'If you are, then leave everything to me. Don't worry. It'll all blow over.'

Bethany couldn't share his optimism. 'Any plan involving deceiving Harland Somerville does not fill me with confidence.'

'In our business, this sort of thing happens every day.'

'It doesn't do to mess with Harland Somerville, Anthony, and I speak from experience.'

'He's nothing more than a bag of wind,' was his robust response. 'What's he ever done in life?'

'He does have a powerful uncle.'

'Sam isn't going to abandon filming now. We're over halfway through, and I've heard the stills are setting the screen on fire. We could have a hit on our hands, and there's even talk about awards. That's why that creepy reporter was so keen to get his photo. Everyone wants a piece of the action. Sam Richards is back on the scene and he's hot news.'

Anthony's reassurance eased the butterflies dancing a tango in Bethany's stomach and she began to relax.

'Sally will give the Catriona scheme her full support, believe me,' Anthony insisted. 'And as I'd do anything to protect my family, it's winners all round.'

'Sally's a lucky girl,' Bethany said.

'I'm the lucky one,' Anthony insisted. 'That's why I'm determined not to let anything upset her.' He glanced over Bethany's shoulder. 'That's my call.'

Sam wedged himself between them. 'If you two have quite finished whispering, you're needed on set, Anthony.'

'Speak to you later, Bethany.' Anthony ambled off to where a make-up girl was applying a powder puff to Catriona's cheeks in an effort to tone down her heightened colour. Another assistant was busy arranging the lace fichu on her gown to best effect. As he passed by, Anthony murmured soothing words in Catriona's ear. She turned to him with a grateful smile, then cast a shy glance in Bethany's direction.

'That's better,' Johnny Morton encouraged from behind his camera. 'Makes my job a lot easier when you relax, Catriona. More sweet nothings please, Anthony.'

Still blushing furiously, Catriona lowered her eyes.

Wendel sidled in through the library

door. He was wearing a new jumper, and the tawny autumn shades emphasised his hazel eyes. 'Can I watch?' he asked.

'Only if you remain absolutely silent,' Sam said in a no-nonsense voice.

'I won't move,' Wendel promised. Then, catching sight of Lottie, he blew her a kiss. The gesture earned a look of reproof from Sam. 'Sorry. I'll sit on my hands.' He settled down on a corner chair.

'You seem to have overcome your aversion to our leading lady,' Bethany spoke in a low voice.

'Lottie's not such a bad old bird.' Wendel's complexion was beginning to match his jumper.

'That's new, isn't it?' Bethany asked. 'The jumper?'

'Present from Lottie,' he mumbled.

'Is it indeed?' Bethany raised her eyebrows.

'Haven't you got anything better to do than sit around commenting on my wardrobe?' Wendel snapped.

Sam turned to face the pair of them. 'Where are Bouncer and the rabbits?' he demanded.

'Bouncer's asleep in the kitchen,' Wendel informed him, 'and I've been assured that the latch on the rabbit hutch has been secured.'

'Right then, if we're all ready.' Sam stood up. A hush descended on the crew. 'Action.'

In the darkness of the drawing room, the scene was set for the confrontation between Lottie, Anthony and Catriona. 'I know what it's like to be in love,' Lottie said to Anthony as she swept across the room, 'and I'm not talking about your father.'

'My father was the love of your life,' Anthony insisted.

'I did grow to love the duke eventually, but he wasn't my first love. My first love was an army officer. We were unable to marry. My parents forbade it. Then when he died — ' Lottie's voice grew husky. ' — I thought my heart would never mend.'

'This is different.'

'Is it?' Lottie raised a disbelieving eyebrow.

'You can't possibly understand what I feel for Elena.'

'I understand more than you will ever know.'

Throughout the exchange, Catriona cowered in a corner. Lottie now looked her up and down.

'Come here, *mon enfant*.' Displaying all the gallantry of his class, Anthony offered Catriona his arm and escorted her to where Lottie was now seated on her favourite chair. She tapped her fan on the fine French upholstery, indicating that Catriona should take the seat beside her.

'You're very young.' There was a hint of compassion in the older woman's voice.

'Elena's eighteen, the same age you were when you married Father,' Anthony put in.

'I'm sure Elena can speak for herself.'

'I do love your son,' Catriona said

after a short pause.

'Enough to give him up?' Lottie asked.

Catriona lowered her eyes. A tear trickled down her cheek. Everyone in the room held their breath. Wiping it away with the back of her hand, Catriona tossed back her head. It was all Bethany could do not to gasp. She was beautiful.

'If you can give up the love of your life, your grace, then so can I.'

The look of sympathy Lottie cast Catriona didn't need words. All the emotions were there — pity, gratitude and admiration tinged with reluctant respect. 'Thank you,' she whispered.

'Cut!' Sam shouted at the same moment that Wendel broke into a vigorous round of applause.

'Fantastic, Lottie!' He jumped to his feet, then sat down again as everyone cast appalled looks in his direction. 'Forgot myself. Sorry.'

'If we can't edit out the interruption, we're going to have to go for a re-shoot,' Sam said in a weary voice.

'Nonsense. I'm sure something can be done.' Lottie cast Sam her best leading-lady smile. 'And I couldn't bear to re-shoot. I'm exhausted. Merrill, deal with this wig before I get one of my headaches and sue Richards Productions for giving me migraines. Only joking.' She cast a coquettish smile at Sam.

Sam's response was far from responsive.

'Listen up please, everyone.' Lottie clapped her hands. 'As this is my last day's filming,' she continued, addressing the room, 'there will be drinks and nibbles in The Goose and Galleon this evening. You're all invited. Partners welcome.' A round of applause greeted her announcement. 'Now will someone please relieve me of this whalebone corset before I crack a rib?'

As Lottie was ushered off the set, the room was plunged into darkness. 'Not again,' a voice groaned.

'Catriona,' Bethany heard Anthony's

voice, 'give me your hand. We don't want you falling over.'

'I'm already there,' Johnny Morton said. 'It's this way, Catriona, and watch out for the cables.'

'Can somebody sort this out please?' another voice said, raised in exasperation.

'It's probably an overloaded fuse.' Wendel flashed a torch around the room.

'Where did you get that?' Sam demanded.

'There's one in every room for emergencies. Power cuts aren't that unusual in this part of the world, especially when the weather's bad and our wiring plays up. It's best to be prepared. Angel,' he said, flickering his torch at Bethany, 'why don't you show Sam the fuse box?'

Bethany did not relish the idea of going down to the cold room with only Sam Richards for company. 'Why me and why Sam?' she hissed.

'Because I have things to sort out here.'

'Like finding us all a torch,' Anthony called out. 'We need to raid your secret stash, Wendel. The light on my mobile phone is about to give out.'

'Off you go.' Wendel shooed Bethany off in the direction of the cold room. 'Someone in the crew ought to know where the fuse box is. Sam, I nominate you. Let me bribe you with my torch.'

'It's this way,' Bethany gave in with as much good grace as she could muster.

'I'll keep an eye on things for you up here,' Wendel said. 'And make sure no one starts telling ghost stories.'

Lottie, divested of her wig and corset, was now wearing a casual shirt and leggings. 'You know, this reminds me of a film I was in. It was set in World War Two, and the director, who looked as though he should still have been at school, insisted on realism. We all had to grope around in the dark. I've never seen so many bruised shins in my life. The poor darling received a few home truths that day, and some were delivered in very colourful language.'

Sam grabbed Bethany's hand. His fingers intertwined with hers. 'Not afraid of the dark, are you?'

'Of course not,' she retaliated. 'And you don't have to come down to the cold room with me. I can draw you a map of where the fuse box is situated, or I could take one of the electricians with me.'

Bethany's eyes began to adjust to the darkness. Sam was looking intently at her. 'We need to talk,' he said in a quiet voice.

'This is hardly the moment,' Bethany began to protest, 'and we've already had our talk this morning.'

'I should imagine there will be no one else in this cold room of yours, and I have one or two things I need to say to you. Now come on.'

10

'If this is about Harland, or Anthony and me playing in the snow, then I've said all I'm going to say on the matter,' Bethany began, but got no further.

'First things first,' insisted Sam. 'Where's this fuse box?'

'Over there.' Bethany flashed her torch in the direction of the far wall.

'Got it. Thank goodness it's a modern one. I didn't fancy dealing with one of those old-fashioned things. We could've been here all day.'

'It's the only part of the electrics Wendel could afford to have renovated — and you didn't really have to deal with it at all. I could have done it on my own.'

'Stop lecturing me and bring that torch closer.' Sam stretched up to slide open the panel. Bethany could feel his arms straining against hers as he reached up to the controls. 'Here goes. Hold your breath.' Sam flicked a switch. The cold room was instantly bathed in harsh electric light. 'Success.' They blinked at each other to a background of faint cheers.

Bethany turned off her torch and put it down on an adjacent shelf. 'Wendel should really have seen to it, but he's very good at getting other people to do his dirty work.'

'At least we got the right switch.' Sam slid the panel shut and dusted his hands. He looked round the shelves cluttered with buckets and empty bottles and wrinkled his nose. 'Can you smell sour milk?'

'They used to churn the milk for cheeses and butter in here in the old days. That's why the walls are white — at least, they used to be. No one's bothered to paint them in years.'

'I think the ceiling's moulting.' Sam brushed flecks of faded white paint out of his hair.

'Right, well, if we're finished here . . . '

'We're not.' Sam put out a hand to detain Bethany.

'I can't keep saying I'm sorry about the snowball fight with Anthony. Can we draw a line under the matter if I promise not to do it again?'

In the squashed surroundings of the cold room there wasn't much space to move away from Sam. It was a heady experience, and one Bethany was beginning to find unsettling. 'Can we rejoin the others?'

'Not yet,' Sam insisted.

'I think we should, before they start gossiping about what's taking us so long.'

'I said we need to talk, and that's exactly what we're going to do. No one will disturb us here, and we may never get another chance to talk in private. I need to know about you and Harland Somerville.'

Bethany wasn't sure if the cold wall supporting her or the mention of Harland's name was the cause of the chilling sensation creeping up her backbone. 'Why?'

'Indulge me?' The stark light bulb

dangling from the ceiling highlighted the amber flecks in Sam's hazel eyes.

'I'm sure Leo's filled you in on all the details. But if you want to make sure our stories gel, I met Harland when I was working for his uncle. At first I was flattered by his interest in me. When he turns on the charm he's a difficult man to resist.'

'Go on,' Sam urged when she lapsed into silence. 'You have my full attention.'

'I'm embarrassed to admit I was foolish enough to put my name to something I shouldn't have. To this day I don't recall the document details, but I was implicated in some of Harland's business dealings. I've been told they weren't exactly illegal.'

'But under scrutiny they wouldn't come out too well?'

'Something along those lines. Anyway, the transactions were discovered when one of Leo Somerville's junior accountants was doing an annual audit. Leo tackled Harland about it . . . ' Bethany's throat dried up. ' . . . and I didn't have a leg to stand on.'

'Harland covered his tracks?'

'Everything Leo said about me was true. It was my name on the documents. I was the one responsible for signing off the transaction. Of course if I'd had a team of expensive lawyers fighting my case, I could possibly have wriggled out of things. But I didn't.'

'I presume Harland kept his name out it?'

'It was put to me that if I didn't resign I would be dismissed. I tried to stand up for myself, but Harland tells a good story, and we were dealing with his uncle. Leo was adamant. One way or another I had to leave. I didn't really want to stay on anyway. I knew I had no future working for the Somervilles. I hadn't seen or heard from Harland until he turned up here with Catriona Cleeve.'

'I think you've misjudged Leo Somerville.'

'Of course you're going to take his

side,' Bethany flared up. 'Everybody else did, so why should you be any different? Money talks.'

'He's not as black as you paint him.'

'He couldn't be.' Bethany's jaw tightened.

'Have you ever thought that he did you a favour?'

'I fail to see how.'

'Would you have gone on trusting Harland if that accountant hadn't blown the whistle?'

Bethany blinked. 'I don't know,' she confessed.

'Leo may have suspected what Harland was up to. By dismissing you, he put a stop to the scheme and at the same time got you safely out of Harland's way.'

'By ruining my reputation? Have you any idea what you're talking about?'

'I'm glad this room's got thick walls.' Sam patted the brickwork. 'No one can hear us. But I suggest you keep your voice down an octave or two unless you want everyone to know your business.'

'I've long ago given up caring what people think about me. I know I'm innocent of any wrongdoing and that's all that matters to me. By the way, I'm not sure Wendel knows the full details, so I'd be grateful if you didn't mention anything to him.'

'Your secret is safe with me.'

Bethany picked up her torch. It gave her something to do to stop her hands from shaking. 'It's not a secret, but I don't want him knowing, that's all,' she said, not looking at Sam. 'He'd be . . .' She searched for the right word. 'Disappointed.'

'I understand.' Sam's voice was as soft as hers.

Bethany wished he wouldn't look at her quite so sympathetically. 'And if you think I enjoy playing the victim, I don't. When things go wrong and I'm at fault, I'm prepared to admit it, but when it's unjust I am not going to sit down and say nothing.'

'No one's accusing you of anything. Calm down,' Sam insisted. 'We don't want Wendel barging in and challenging me to a duel.'

Bethany gave a shamefaced smile. 'I suppose mention of the Somerville name still has the power to send me over the top. Anyway, what is your involvement with Leo Somerville?' she asked. 'Why are you so keen to stick up for him?'

'To repeat your words, money talks.'

Bethany's lip curled in disbelief. For all his fine words, Sam was no better than the Somervilles. 'I see.' Her voice was as cold as the brickwork.

'No, you don't. And before you jump down my throat, at least give me a chance to explain.'

'You don't have to tell me anything. I've heard enough for one day.'

Sam ignored her. 'Leo Somerville is providing financial backing for *Love Will Find a Way*.'

'That's not news to me.'

'What you may not know is that after a long break it's almost impossible to get back into the swing of things. It's true of any business and filming is no different. I was having a tough time getting anyone to even listen to me. I was beginning to despair, then Leo Somerville set up some meetings and interviews. He generated interest in the project. Soon he had an impressive list of sponsors on board. He worked hard on my behalf, and for that I'm grateful. There's also some other stuff between us, but we'll leave that for another time.'

'How do you think Leo's going to react when he learns about my involvement in his project?'

'He knows already.'

'Of course — Harland will have told him.'

'And it isn't Harland's project, it's mine. Leo trusts my judgement and is content to take a back seat.'

'Unless Harland starts stirring things up again.'

'He won't. Harland has no control over filming, but his uncle feels that it's a good idea to let him think he has.'

'Why?'

'You've heard the old saying about keeping your friends close and your enemies closer still?'

'Harland and Leo aren't enemies.'

'No, but Leo likes to keep an eye on his nephew.'

'Then I hope your confidence in Leo isn't misplaced.'

'For my part, I have every trust in Leo. There are things about him you don't know.'

'I know he'll always stick up for his nephew. I'm living proof of that.'

'He has a lot to lose if the film bombs.'

Sam took Bethany's face in his hands. The pale mark on his ring finger was fading but it stood as a reminder that somewhere, some time he had been in a serious relationship. Bethany also couldn't shake off the suspicion that Sam's mysterious professional absence had something to do with Leo Somerville. Why else would Sam be so fiercely protective of his sponsor and

Leo equally as supportive of Sam?

'Sam, what is the point of this private talk?' she demanded.

'We needed to clear the air between us.'

'But we haven't.'

'I wouldn't say that.'

'We're going round in circles.' Bethany stiffened in resistance as Sam moved in closer.

'Bethany what would you say if . . . ' he began to ask.

'Sam?' a voice called out.

'Now what?' Sam raised his eyes in exasperation.

'You're needed up here.'

Bethany twisted her face away from Sam's. 'We're checking the fuses. We'll be out in a minute.'

'The publicity people have arrived.'

'I'd better go and see what they want,' Sam muttered. 'Come on.'

Bethany's legs shook as she followed Sam out of the cold room. There was so much about him she didn't know, and whatever he had wanted to say to her still hadn't been said. It could only be something to do with the Somervilles, and that part of her life was most definitely closed. Why then did she feel she could trust Sam Richards? It didn't make sense.

'There you are,' Merrill Sims said as they emerged from the cold room. 'Anthony and Catriona are on the terrace having their pictures taken. Sorry, Bethany, but Anthony has transferred his affections to the leading lady. You are so yesterday.'

'That's the best bit of news I've had all day.' Bethany greeted her words with a smile of relief as Sam was accosted by a member of the publicity team. 'Anything else?' she asked Merrill.

Johnny Morton appeared in the doorway. 'Two things.'

Bethany looked at the expression on his face with a sense of foreboding.

'The rabbits have had a major falling out and wrecked the hutch.'

'And?' she asked with a weary sigh.

'I've saved the best bit til last.

Lottie's cried off tonight's party.'

'That's not possible.'

'I can assure you it is.'

'But before the lights went out, she was full of it.'

'That's showbiz for you.' Johnny grinned. 'The canapés and drinks will be there, but Lottie won't be gracing us with her presence.'

'Why not?'

'She said she had another urgent call. Wendel's taken her to the station.'

'On the back of his bike?' Bethany didn't think she could take any more shocks.

'No,' Johnny said patiently, 'in his fifties roadster. We had to push it out of the barn.'

'That old death trap?'

'It took some starting up, I can tell you, but Lottie was great. She helped push.'

'I suppose I should be glad she and Wendel have put their differences behind them.'

'They were getting on like a house on

fire, cracking jokes and swapping reminiscences. You should've heard them.'

'Perhaps it's as well I didn't,' Bethany sighed, adding, 'Thanks for the update.'

'My pleasure.'

Johnny glanced over his shoulder. 'It looks like the publicity boys have finished.'

Catriona detached herself from the group on the terrace and headed towards them.

'Anything we can do for you?' Johnny greeted her.

'Are we still on for Lottie's party?' Catriona asked. 'I want to thank her for helping me with that last scene. She gave me some great advice.'

'Lottie's not going to be th ... ' Bethany began, then winced as Johnny crushed her toes with his work boots.

'I'll be there,' he promised.

Catriona's face lit up. 'I'm looking forward to it already.'

Intrigued, Bethany looked from one to the other.

'Weren't you going to go and see to your rabbits?' Johnny directed a pointed look at Bethany.

'Rabbits?' Catriona took a step backwards, a worried frown creasing her brow.

'They can wait,' Bethany teased, then took pity on the pair of them. 'Perhaps I should go and see what's happening. Catch up with you later.'

As Bethany moved away, something shiny caught her eye. She bent down to pick it up off the carpet. It was Sam's lapel pin displaying the red dragon logo.

11

When Wendel didn't put in an appearance at Lottie's party at The Goose and
Galleon, Bethany had not been unduly
worried. Late nights and loud music
weren't exactly his thing. The evening
had been a riotous success, and the film
crew weren't going to let the absence of
the hostess spoil a good party.

Bethany hadn't returned to Waterbridge Manor until well after midnight.
She had expected to find Wendel dozing
in front of his coal fire. He usually
waited up for her whenever she went
out, but there had been no sign of him
in the library. Deciding he must have
gone to bed, Bethany had tapped on his
bedroom door and called out 'good
night' before making her way to her
own room. It was only when Wendel
didn't come down for breakfast and
Bethany went to check up on him that

she realised his bed hadn't been slept in.

'He can't disappear into thin air,' Sam insisted.

'You don't know Wendel.'

Harbouring some vague idea that Wendel had perhaps taken Bouncer for an early morning walk, Bethany had gone back down to the kitchen to find the dog scratching at the conservatory door, eager to go outside. After telephoning Sam, who had promised to join her, immediately she'd grabbed Bouncer's lead and headed for the lake. Her ears were now stinging with cold. She thrust her hands deep into the pockets of the old coat she was wearing, annoyed that Sam seemed unaffected by the chill wind blowing off the lake.

'Has he done anything like this before?' he asked.

'Once or twice,' Bethany was forced to admit. 'He and Mary led an unconventional life. They travelled the world and occasionally they would take off together. They were free spirits and didn't like to make plans.'

'Well then, surely we've nothing to worry about.'

Bethany wiped the back of her hand across her face, an inelegant gesture but one she hoped would help clear the jumble of thoughts racing round her head. 'He's never left me in the lurch before.'

'And I'm sure he hasn't this time.'

Bethany stamped her feet in an effort to revive her circulation.

'Let's walk,' Sam suggested. 'Maybe the morning air will clear our heads.'

Bethany's feet slipped on the wet wood of the stile leading down to the lake. Sam clamped his arms around her body and lowered her safely back to the ground. 'That thing's lethal.' His eyes pierced hers as he looked down at her.

'Thank you,' Bethany mumbled, wondering if she would sound ungrateful if she told Sam that all she now really wanted was to be alone.

For a few moments they trudged on in silence, their laboured breathing and the clump of their heavy boots the only sounds to break the silence.

'You don't have any plans to take off after Wendel, do you?' Sam eventually asked.

'It'd serve him right if I did,' Bethany replied.

'Please don't.'

Bethany ignored the flutter of pleasure his words stirred up in her chest, but knew there were more important issues at stake here than having her head turned by Sam Richards begging her to stay. 'What if something's happened to Wendel?' she asked.

Sam winced from the pressure of Bethany's clenched fingers circling his wrist. 'I'm sure nothing has.'

'He always drives far too fast in that old car of his, and the roads are treacherous in places. Supposing he's skidded off somewhere and is lying unconscious in a ditch?'

'I think we would've heard something by now if that was the case.'

'Do you think I ought to contact the

police? Or ring round the local hospitals?'

'Bethany,' Sam said as he placed his hands on her shoulders, 'chill out.'

'It's all very well for you — Wendel's not your godfather.' Bethany's sobs caught in her throat. 'I can't help thinking the worst. He's not been himself lately.'

'What do you mean?'

'Having a garden party in the snow? You've got to admit that's odd by anybody's standards.'

'Didn't you enjoy it?'

'That's not the point.'

'Then what is?'

'He's been behaving out of character. I mean, inviting a film crew to stay?'

'Technically that's not correct. We're not staying with him,' Sam pointed out. 'And didn't I hear somewhere that he and Mary loved company?'

'Yes, but . . . ' Bethany ran a hand through her hair. 'I'm confused,' she admitted. 'What do you think has happened to him?'

'If you want my opinion, I think he's probably with Lottie.'

'Doing what?' Bethany demanded.

'Well, they were both last seen driving off together in his car.' Sam paused delicately. 'They're mature adults. We know they have history.' He raised his eyebrows at Bethany.

She blinked as the full meaning of Sam's words sunk in. 'Are you saying what I think you're saying?'

'It's a logical assumption.'

'No it isn't.' Bethany was vehement.

'Watch your step,' Sam cautioned as her feet threatened to slide from under her.

'Wendel was devoted to Mary.'

'I'm not saying otherwise.'

Bethany could feel the warmth of Sam's body against hers as she regained her balance. She forced herself to take a step backwards. Getting too close to Sam Richards was a dangerous course of action, and right now she was too vulnerable to deal with any more onslaughts of her senses.

'Are you forgetting Wendel hid away from Lottie in his library because he didn't want commitment?'

'Maybe he's had a rethink. Lottie can be one persuasive lady.'

'I don't know what to make of anything anymore,' Bethany admitted.

'My advice is that for the time being we sit this one out.'

'We can't carry on as if nothing's happened. Wendel has responsibilities. He needs to be here.'

'We can carry on without him, but you need to be here.'

'I don't see why I should,' Bethany said with a mutinous toss of her head. 'I'm as mad as a box of frogs. I should've known Wendel would do something like this.'

She felt like shoving Sam in the chest. He had no right to look so together when her world was falling apart. 'Why shouldn't I take off like everyone else?'

'Because you have responsibilities.' Sam paused before saying in a rush,

'And you need to be here for insurance purposes.'

'What are you talking about?'

'Your name's on the policy as second nominee. If Wendel is absent for any reason, you have to be on the premises while filming is in progress.'

'My name's what?' Bethany screeched.

'Steady on.'

'Why should I steady on?' Bethany began to feel sick. 'You only want me to stay on for your wretched film. Is that it? You're not covered insurance-wise if I take off too?'

'Wendel didn't tell you about the policy?'

'Too right he didn't.' Bethany was ready to explode.

Sam did his best to pacify her. 'Perhaps he meant to.'

'Whether he meant to or not, his behaviour's unethical. This is exactly what Harland Somerville did to me, only this time I wasn't foolish enough to sign anything, so your wretched policy isn't worth the paper it's written on.'

'You won't have to do anything. You only have to be here. There's nothing to worry about.'

'There's everything to worry about. Wendel's disappeared, and now it seems he's named me on a document that I never knew existed.'

'I know it's a big ask,' Sam said, 'but we only have a few more days of filming left. Can you keep a lid on things until then? I'll make it up to you,' he coaxed.

'How?' Bethany was in no mood to compromise.

'If Wendel hasn't reappeared after filming is finished, I'll find him. How about that?'

'Right now I don't care if I never see him again.'

'You don't mean that.'

'Don't I?' Bethany glared at Sam, then sagged as the fight went out of her. 'You're right, I don't. But how did this happen?'

'Life's full of dirty tricks, but things generally sort themselves out in the end.'

Bethany snapped her fingers. 'The car.'

Sam recoiled from the suddenness of her movement. 'What?'

'Wendel wouldn't leave it unattended at the station.'

'Why not?'

'In case it got vandalised. He hasn't brought it back, so what's happened to it?'

'Then I'm right. He and Lottie have taken off. Problem solved.' Sam appeared to be losing interest in the topic of Wendel's disappearance.

'Where have they gone?'

'That I don't know, and until Wendel contacts us there's nothing further we can do.'

'Doesn't Lottie have any family or friends who might be worried about her?'

'I could contact her agent to see if he's heard anything, but I doubt she's been in touch with him. She's always been notoriously independent.'

Bethany bent down and, picking up a

stray branch that had been blown down in the recent storm, she threw it as far as she could.

'Bethany.' Sam took a step towards her.

'Don't.' She flinched, suspecting he was going to touch her, then added, 'I think I'd like to continue the walk on my own.'

Sam put out a hand to detain her. She tried to shake him off, but Sam's grip was too strong. Turning her face away from him, she caught sight of a silhouetted figure in the distance walking slowly around the far side of the lake.

'Wendel?' she called out, struggling free from Sam's hold.

'That isn't Wendel.' Sam sounded annoyed.

'Then who is it?'

'You don't need me to tell you.'

More confused than ever, Bethany looked back to the approaching figure.

'I'll leave you to your walk.' Sam emphasised the word *walk*. 'If you do decide to see things through, you know where to find me, but don't take too long coming to a decision.'

Feeling as though she was being torn in two directions, Bethany watched him stride away from her. Bouncer barked and began racing towards the new arrival.

'Hi,' Anthony called out and waved at Bethany. 'Glad I caught you. There's something urgent I have to tell you.'

12

'Not now, Anthony. I've had it up to here with everyone's problems.'

'Is that Sam sloping off?' He peered over Bethany's shoulder.

'Yes.'

'Did he recognise me?' he asked with an anxious look.

'He did, and he thinks we've got an assignation.'

'A what?'

'A secret meeting.'

'He's right. I need to talk to you — in secret.'

Bethany's lungs hurt from the effort of breathing so hard. 'Whatever you have to say can wait,' she said firmly.

'No it can't.'

'Not now, Anthony.'

Anthony detained Bethany by grabbing the sleeve of her coat. 'It's Sally.'

'What about her?'

'I need to take a break from filming. Not for long; a few days, no more. You can clear my absence with Sam for me, can't you?'

'No, I can't.'

'Yes you can. You're brilliant at sorting things out.'

'Why can't you contact your agent and tell her? It's her responsibility to deal with this kind of thing.'

'She might think I was being precious.'

'And she'd be absolutely right.'

'Won't you at least try to help me?' Anthony employed his best matinee-idol smile.

'No.'

'I helped you when Catriona stepped in to take your place over that snowball business.'

Bethany could not believe what she was hearing. 'Catriona helped us both.'

'How about you tell Sam I'm worried about structural damage on set?'

'Structural damage?' Bethany was growing more confused by the minute.

'Everyone in the industry is hyper about being sued. Imagine what'd happen if there was an accident because the proper checks hadn't been carried out.'

Bethany now began to experience a slight feeling of distaste. 'Apart from all the other objections I've come up with,' she said slowly and carefully, 'I don't think that Sam would believe me if I told him you were off work because you were scared that the roof was about to fall in.'

'The roof may very well fall in if schedules are disrupted.'

'Not my problem. Now if you'll excuse me, I have things to do. In case you haven't heard, Wendel is missing.'

'Right.' Wrapped up in his own world, Anthony obviously hadn't registered a word Bethany had said. 'What if I persuade my mother-in-law to look after Bouncer during filming? Would that change your mind? He's always getting you into trouble, isn't he?'

'There won't be any filming if you

don't get back on set.'

'Perhaps I didn't explain things very well.' The eager look was back on Anthony's face. 'You see, I can't leave Sally on her own. We're coming to a crucial time.'

'Her mother's with her, isn't she?'

'Kiara's proving a handful.'

'I'm sure Sally's mother won't desert her daughter or her granddaughter in their hour of need. And if nothing else, think of your career,' Bethany added, trying to appeal to Anthony's better nature. 'You've got the starring role. It's your big chance. You can't throw everything away.'

'I thought you'd understand.' He sounded like a spoilt child. 'I know I sound selfish, but I haven't told you the full story.'

'I've heard enough.' Bethany made to walk off, but Anthony detained her.

'I've been trying to make allowances for Sally's mood swings but it hasn't been easy. She's taken it into her head that Catriona and I really do have something going between us.'

'You said they were friends and that she went along with the pretence.'

'She did initially, but Sally's not feeling herself right now. The slightest thing sets her off. I'm trying to do my best for everyone but it's not easy. My mother-in-law thinks I should spend more time with Sally. She's never really approved of her daughter marrying an actor. I'm in an impossible situation.'

The theme tune to Anthony's television series interrupted them. Turning his back on Bethany, he whisked his mobile phone out of his pocket. Not wanting to listen in, Bethany distanced herself from the call. The full circuit of the lake was over a two-mile round trip. The forecast had suggested further snow showers and the wind had changed direction. Bethany shivered from a mixture of cold and apprehension.

Anthony finished his call. 'That was Sally's mother on the line. Sally's been admitted to hospital.' His voice threatened to give out on him.

'For heaven's sake,' Bethany urged, aware that this latest development put a different light on the situation, 'go.'

'What about Sam?'

'I'll square things with him some-how.'

'You can tell him I'm married if it'd make life easier.' Anthony was already moving away from her. 'You have my permission to tell whoever you like. Bouncer,' he called out, 'heel.'

'No, he can stay with me.' Bethany tried to clutch Bouncer's collar, but he was too quick for her. He skipped away towards Anthony.

'A promise is a promise. I said we'd look after him and we will. He can distract Kiara from all that's going on.'

Barking excitedly, Bouncer evaded Bethany's attempts to restrain him and raced off after Anthony. Bethany watched them go. It was only after they'd disappeared from sight that she remembered Anthony's mobile number was a closely guarded secret. She had no way of contacting him or any idea when she would see him again.

The wind now began to smell of snow. Bethany abandoned her plans to walk around the lake even though she desperately needed to clear her head. If Wendel hadn't returned home, she didn't know what she was going to do, but she was sorely tempted to follow everyone else's example and walk off set. Hunching her shoulders and burying her nose in her scarf, she headed back towards Waterbridge Manor.

The house appeared calm and peaceful in the fading light. Bethany pushed opened the gate that led to the house from the kitchen garden. The grass rustled and made a peculiar growling noise. Further inspection revealed Furry hunched up in a tight ball and looking ready for a fight. Bethany bent forward and scooped him up.

'Stop it,' she protested as he wriggled in her arms. Bethany winced from the strength of his struggles as he tried to bite her. 'I don't know what's the matter with everybody today.'

As she strode towards the conservatory, a shadow moved behind the blinds. 'Wendel? Is that you?' she called out.

'It's me.' Johnny Morton poked his head out of the window. 'Hope I didn't scare you.'

'What are you doing here?'

'I'm meeting up with Catriona. I let Furry out because I didn't want him setting off her allergies; then he ran away from me. I see you've found him.'

'Why are you meeting Catriona here?'

'We didn't want everyone knowing that we were planning on taking off for a few hours. We've been discreet, but . . . ' Johnny shrugged. 'You know how it is. Someone's always where they shouldn't be, they spot you together, and the next moment you're tabloid headlines.'

'Look, do you mind if I put Furry back in his hutch? He's normally so amenable, but today he's playing up.'

'That's because he's pregnant.'

Furry delivered another unfriendly growl as Bethany almost dropped him in shock.

She looked down at the reproachful brown eyes fixed firmly on her in an unblinking stare, the whiskers twitching with indignation.

'Here, let me,' Johnny offered. 'Why don't you make us some coffee? White, no sugar please.'

Bethany was spooning coffee into two mugs when Johnny reappeared. 'Is this some kind of joke?' she demanded.

'Sorry, don't follow.'

'Buck rabbits do not have babies.'

'Furry is a doe. She's displaying the classic symptoms of pregnancy. They don't like being stroked or petted; that's why she turned on you. Didn't they tell you what sex she was when you picked her up?'

'No, and I didn't notice.'

'Is that so?' Johnny cast Bethany a disbelieving look. 'Would you like me to take her over to my sister later? She'll sort everything out.'

'Thank you,' Bethany said, feeling rather foolish.

'Right. Sorted. Now come and sit

down and drink your coffee before it gets cold.' Johnny nudged the packet of biscuits at her. 'You look as though you could use one of these too.'

Bethany took one and stared at it thoughtfully.

'Catriona's late,' Johnny observed. 'I hope she's not being held up by Anthony Granger. He's too fond of intimate chats if you ask me. The man's turning into a pest.' Johnny glanced at his watch. 'I wonder if I ought to give her a call.'

'I shouldn't think she's with Anthony. In fact I know she isn't.'

'How can you be sure?' Johnny snatched another biscuit out of the packet.

'I've just left him by the lake.'

'You know something, don't you?' Johnny's eyes narrowed.

Bethany steadied her nerves by clasping her coffee mug with both hands. 'Anthony is married.'

Johnny coughed on his biscuit. 'Are you sure?'

'I found out by accident that day I took a walk in the snow. I bumped into him. It was his daughter I was playing snowballs with when that photographer was hiding in the trees.'

'I didn't see a child in any of the photos.'

'Maybe the tree obscured his lens, I don't know, but you're going to have to take my word for it until you speak to Catriona.'

'She's in on it too?'

'She was at college with Anthony's wife.'

'She never said a word.'

'She was sworn to secrecy.'

'And Sam?'

'He doesn't know any of this.'

Johnny whistled under his breath.

'I was with Anthony down by the lake about half an hour ago, and while we were talking he received a call saying Sally has been admitted to hospital. She's expecting their second child. Anthony asked me to cover up for him while he's away because he's not sure exactly what's going on, and I'm not sure if I'm supposed to tell you any of this before I inform Sam of developments but there you have it. I'd be grateful if you didn't discuss it with anyone but Catriona until I've had a chance to talk to Sam.'

'He won't be best pleased to hear Anthony's walked off set.'

'Everyone else seems to be doing it — Wendel, Lottie, the list is growing by the day.'

'Wendel!' Johnny smacked his forehead with the palm of his hand. 'I meant to tell you. Sorry,' he apologised.

'You've heard something?' Bethany sat up straight.

'He's the reason Furry was on the loose.'

'What?'

'He ran off when I went to answer the telephone.'

'Wendel hasn't been in an accident — ?' The biscuits scattered across the table as Bethany grabbed Johnny's arm.

'No, he's fine.'

'Then where is he?'

'You remember when Lottie first walked off set saying the snow was getting to her?' Bethany nodded. 'It was nothing to do with the snow. She went home to get her birth certificate.' Johnny looked at Bethany as if hoping she would interrupt. When she didn't, he carried on, 'There's no easy way to tell you this.'

'Johnny,' Bethany ground out through clenched teeth, 'get on with it.'

'Lottie and Wendel are married.'

13

It was cosy in the snug of The Goose and Galleon. The flames from the coal fire warmed the oak panels of the priest's hole that had reputedly provided refuge for Charles II when he had been on the run from the Roundheads.

Sam sliced into his sea bass. 'How's your fish?' he asked Bethany.

To Bethany's shame, despite all the recent drama her appetite hadn't deserted her. 'It's delicious,' she admitted, dipping a minted new potato into the watercress sauce.

'Then let's drink a toast.' Sam raised his glass. 'Truce?' he suggested.

'Agreed.' Bethany nodded as they chinked glasses.

'I like to see you smile. You don't do it often enough and that's a pity.'

The flames now did a good job of heightening Bethany's colour. She wished

Sam wouldn't look at her quite so intently.

'There hasn't been much to smile about recently,' she managed to reply.

'I disagree,' was Sam's calm response.

'How can you say that?' Bethany protested, then bit her lip, aware that she sounded snappy.

'Eat up,' Sam urged her, 'before your food gets cold. Then maybe you won't feel so much like arguing on a full stomach.'

'I'm not arguing,' Bethany began, then backed down, seeing the teasing light in Sam's eyes. 'Have it your own way,' she sighed.

'As it's rude to speak with your mouth full, I have to tell you there's plenty to smile about.'

Bethany speared a buttered baby carrot. George prided himself on his cooking and tonight he had excelled himself. The demands on the kitchen had been heavy over the past few weeks and she was glad he hadn't let standards slip.

'There's Wendel's news for a start,' Sam said.

Word of his marriage had spread like wildfire, she thought.

Sam gave her a shrewd look. 'You don't seem surprised by developments.'

Bethany dabbed at her mouth with her paper tissue before replying. 'I gave up being surprised by anything Wendel did ages ago. It saves time, and at least we now don't need to scour the countryside or make frantic telephone calls to the police.'

'Do you know where Wendel is?' Sam asked.

'I received a text from Lottie saying how happy she was and that she hoped they had my blessing.'

'Nothing from Wendel?'

'He funked it.'

'He's going to have to face up to you sometime.'

'When he does, I'll have more than a few words to say to him.'

'I wonder why he and Lottie didn't tell anyone what they were up to,' Sam mused.

'Wendel must have thought I would

try to talk him out of it.'

'And would you?'

'Probably.'

'Then there's our answer.'

'Maybe, but would it really have hurt him and Lottie to wait a little longer until filming was finished?'

'I suppose not,' Sam agreed.

'It's always the same with Wendel. He creates chaos, then expects everyone to pick up the pieces after him.'

Sam looked thoughtful 'Do you know, I don't think Lottie's ever been married before. She's had several near misses, but her career always came first. Maybe that's why she didn't want to wait, in case Wendel got cold feet like he did all those years ago.'

'Well she'll have her hands full with Wendel. She can have that bit of advice for free.'

'Nothing Lottie won't be able to cope with, but what about you?'

'Me?'

'You don't mind staying on at Waterbridge Manor without Wendel?'

'Do I have any choice?'

'You do of course,' Sam conceded, then raised his eyebrows at her, 'but there is a lot riding on the final few days of filming.'

'I won't let you down.'

Sam's quirky smile lit up his face. 'Words to warm my heart. And let's hope Wendel will be back soon.'

'I haven't dared tell my mother.'

Sam's hand was warm as he squeezed hers. 'I'll make it up to you, I promise, once filming is finished.'

'And Anthony?' Bethany forced herself to ask, pushing all thoughts of future activities with Sam to the back of her mind.

His hazel eyes softened in the light of the fire. 'Ah yes, Anthony. I wondered when we'd get round to talking about him. It seems I owe you an apology.'

'Is that why you suggested this dinner?'

'We needed to talk, and as I know you have a healthy appetite, I thought dinner would be a good idea. Also, I have to admit I behaved badly this morning. I should never have thrown a hissy fit.'

'Why did you?' Bethany felt compelled to ask.

'It's a complex situation.'

'What does that mean?'

'You're not going to get an answer right now, but tell me — has Sally had her baby yet?'

Caught off her guard, Bethany's fork clattered onto her plate.

'Steady, you'll spill George's excellent sauce all over the table.' Sam dabbed at the mess with a paper serviette.

'You knew about the baby?' Bethany gulped down an unhealthy mouthful of wine.

'I do now,' Sam agreed solemnly.

'How? I mean, who?'

'You can't keep anything quiet for long in this business. I think Anthony wanted to be found out and that's why he was playing up. I should have realised the situation sooner.'

'What caused you to suspect he was married?'

'The way you were so worried about being identified as the snowballing blonde. I know there was a lot of fuss at the time, but it wasn't that serious an incident.'

'I was worried Sally would think the worst.'

'I presume Catriona was in on the secret too?'

'She knows Anthony's wife, and she wanted to get Harland Somerville off her back, so she offered to take my place as the significant other in Anthony's life.'

Sam nodded. 'And everyone came up with a plan?'

'It seemed a good idea at the time. But you still haven't told me who told you about Sally.'

'Johnny Morton. Don't blame him.' Sam held up a hand before Bethany could speak. 'I overheard him and Catriona discussing what to do. Then when they saw me,' he added with a shrug, 'it all came out.'

'I know I should've told you before anyone else, but my head was all over the place — what with Wendel's news and your suspicions about me and Anthony, and then when Johnny broke the news about Furry being pregnant. That was the final straw.'

'Yet again I've been upstaged by that darned rabbit. There really is something in the air around here, isn't there? Babies, weddings, romances . . . ' Sam cast Bethany a meaningful look.

She lowered her eyes, uncertain how to continue. They ate in silence for a few moments.

'To change the subject completely,' Sam spoke first, 'the advance rushes of *Love Will Find a Way* have received positive feedback, and Leo Somerville advises that the investors are happy. I think we have a hit on our hands.'

'Seriously?'

'You heard it here first.'

'Then what are you going to do?'

'You mean after I've finished filming?'

'I suppose I do,' Bethany replied, surprised by the feeling of loss there would be in her life when she wouldn't be seeing Sam Richards again.

'I sit back and wait for more offers of work to pour in.'

'You've nothing lined up?'

''Fraid not.'

'But your reputation — '

'You're only as good as your last film, and if it bombs no one wants to know you.'

'Aren't you worried about your future?'

A pensive look crossed Sam's face. 'It's all relative, wouldn't you say?'

'I don't understand.'

'There are more important things in life than films.'

Bethany frowned. There were times when Sam Richards didn't add up. Now was one of them.

'I follow the Far Eastern philosophy: take each day as it comes. It wouldn't be the end of the world if I couldn't make another film. That's something my travels have taught me.'

'But you said you came back because you missed the life.'

'I know you're not going to like this, but I missed the money.'

'Sorry to interrupt, Bethany,' George put in. He was hovering by Sam's elbow.

She looked up at him, but with Sam's words still in her head, his face swam in and out of focus. Had she totally misread Sam Richards? Until now she had regarded him as the most unmaterialistic person she knew.

'George,' she queried with a confused frown, 'is something wrong?'

'There's a telephone call. It's Johnny Morton. It sounded urgent.'

'I'll take it.' Sam stood up, signalling for Bethany to stay seated. 'You finish your sea bass.'

Bethany stared down at her plate. She no longer felt hungry.

'How very cosy.' The taunting voice of Harland Somerville rang in her ears. She snapped her head back. He was standing in front of her, smiling as if he were pleased to see her.

'Who would have thought it, you and Sam Richards? Mind if I sit down? Is this a special occasion?'

'What do you want?' Bethany demanded.

'Just playing catch-up. What a lot has been happening in my absence. Is it true Wendel's married?'

'Yes.'

'And to Lisolette St James?'

'They're old friends.'

'If you say so.'

Bethany didn't know why she was bothering to explain things to Harland. He always put his own interpretation on any situation regardless of the truth.

'You know it's a pity you and I never made it together. It's not too late. I'm prepared to put the past behind us if you are. What do you say?'

'What are you doing here?'

'Down to business already?' Harland sighed. 'If you must know, I actually came to see Catriona Cleeve.'

Bethany sliced into another potato

and pretended to eat it, determined not to let Harland's presence upset her.

'What's all this I'm hearing about her and Anthony Granger?' Harland asked.

'What have you heard?'

'That they're more than good friends.'

'Is that so?'

'I thought it was you and Anthony who liked playing snowballs.'

'Which just goes to show you can't believe everything you read in the newspapers, doesn't it?' Bethany pushed away her plate and leaned back in her chair.

'My, aren't you the feisty one?'

Bethany looked at Harland with complete indifference, glad he no longer held the power to control her emotions. 'I believe in standing up for myself.'

'You've changed,' Harland said.

'I had to. You taught me a valuable lesson in life.'

'I would've set things right between us, but you didn't hang around long enough.'

'I wasn't given the option to stay.' Bethany shook her head. 'We're going over old ground. I've moved on, Harland, and I suggest you do the same.'

'If by moving on you mean setting your sights on Sam Richards, I would advise against it.'

Bethany remembered enough about Harland's smile to know he was out to make trouble. 'I haven't set my sights on anyone.'

'That's good, because there's a lot about him you don't know.'

'I'm sure there is,' Bethany agreed.

'For instance, are you aware that he and Uncle Leo have scheduled a visit to Asia after *Love Will Find a Way* finishes filming?'

'Have they?' Bethany effected an unconcerned air. Her stepfather had always told her that in business most people followed the money. It was wise advice. Sam's first loyalty would be to Leo Somerville. Hadn't he admitted he was only interested in filming for the money?

'What exactly has that to do with

me?' she asked Harland.

If he was disappointed by her reaction, he didn't show it. 'Have you never wondered why Sam disappeared so suddenly after his career was set to skyrocket?'

'It really is none of my business.'

'You should make it your business.'

'Why?'

'You may not be quite so keen to be friends with him, that's why.'

'I have no idea what you're talking about.' Bethany looked round, wishing Sam would come back.

'Ask him about The Dragon.'

Bethany stiffened.

'I see you get my drift,' Harland said, noticing her body language. 'It's quite a set-up.'

'What do you know about The Dragon?'

'It's not my place to tell you.'

Her jaw tightened in frustration. Harland knew exactly which buttons to press to spike her curiosity.

'Now,' Harland drawled, glanced at

his elaborate watch, 'much as I am enjoying your company, I have to leave you.' He finished his glass of wine. 'Give my regards to Sam, and tell him I'm sorry I couldn't stay.'

Bethany's relief was coated with irritation. Harland had said just enough to stimulate her interest.

'I'll be seeing you,' he said.

Before he could reach the door, it flew open and crashed back against the wall. 'Steady,' Harland cautioned as Sam re-entered. 'I know you're keen to see Bethany again after having been away from her for all of two minutes, but there's no need to crush the rest of us in your enthusiasm.'

Sam ignored him. 'That was Johnny on the telephone.'

Bethany cast a warning glance in Harland's direction, hoping Sam would be discreet.

'We've got to leave — now.'

'No dessert?' Harland mocked.

Sam continued to address Bethany: 'Waterbridge Manor is on fire.'

14

Sam kick-started the ignition. 'Where's Bouncer?'

'He's with Anthony's mother-in-law, and Johnny's sister has got Furry.' Bethany had to raise her voice above the power of the motorbike revs.

'Then don't forget to wear this.' Sam thrust an orange crash helmet at her. Bethany's fingers were trembling so badly she could hardly do up the strap. 'Ready? Hang on tight.'

Bethany locked her arms around Sam's waist. She could feel him straining his muscles against the surge of the throttle. They shot forward with an angry snarl. She gritted her teeth, dreading to think what damage the potholes would do to the bike's undercarriage. Wendel prided himself on fitting only the finest quality tyres. Bethany prayed they would live up to

180

their advertising slogan that proclaimed they were the best on the road. She ducked as they bumped through showers of muddy slush. Her heart beat a tattoo against Sam's back. His lungs strained for breath against hers.

A ghostly silver moon glided through a break in the clouds, its shadow creating menacing shapes in the darkness. Sam eased up as they approached the crossroads. Bethany stifled a shriek at the sound of a low cough from behind the hedge.

'It's only a cow,' Sam reassured her, adding, 'Lean to the left.'

'What?' Bethany shouted.

'I need you to counter balance my weight, unless you want to wind up in the ditch with a cow trampling you into the mud.'

Bethany closed her eyes and did as she was told. It had been a good few years since she'd ridden on the back of Wendel's bike. Mary didn't think it was a very ladylike activity, and Bethany had gradually grown out of the habit of riding pillion. She hoped Wendel's confidence in Sam's road skills was not misplaced. Stray hawthorn tendrils whipped her legs as she stretched her body sideways in a frantic attempt to keep her balance. Sam was driving like a maniac and she wasn't sure he would even notice if she fell off. Her face stung from the force of the bitter wind, and the moment she began to think she couldn't hold on any longer Sam shouted, 'OK, you can straighten up. The worst part is over.'

Bethany sagged against his back. Her chest felt as though it had suffered a frenzied attack with an ice pick, and her eyelashes were freezing up on her. Her throat too was raw from the battering it had received from the punishing night air.

In the distance she could hear the faint wail of a fire engine.

'Here we go,' Sam shouted.

He didn't bother to slow down for the speed hump, and they almost became airborne as he took it at a higher than recommended speed. Blue lights flashed further down the hill as the rescue services gained on them.

'There's Waterbridge Manor,' Sam shouted into the wind. 'Get ready to jump off.'

Bethany couldn't see a thing. Her eyelids were glued together against the bitter air stream and her legs were shaking with cold and fright. She feared they might not support her as she slid off the back of the pillion seat before Sam had come to a halt. Wendel's expensive tyres hissed in protest and shuddered to a standstill. Bethany landed on her knees on grass saturated by weeks of winter weather. Cold snow seeped through her torn tights as she crawled along in the darkness, her fingers fumbling for the gate. Sam shone his headlight down the drive.

'What can you see?' he called out.

'What?' she called back.

'Take your helmet off.' Sam gestured to her head as Bethany groped around in the mud.

'Bethany, is that you?' A figure loomed at her out of the dark.

'Down here,' she called out as Johnny yanked open the gate.

He dragged her to her feet. 'Where've you been? I've been looking out for you for ages.'

She sobbed against his chest, clinging onto his shoulders in an attempt to steady her shaking legs. 'Is that the emergency services?' he asked. The wail of sirens grew louder.

'Johnny,' Bethany shouted, 'is Waterbridge Manor still standing? Why can't I see any flames?' She pushed him away. 'I have to get to the house.'

'No, don't.' Johnny clamped her body to his chest. 'Catriona raced inside before I could stop her. I'm not having you do the same.'

'What?' Bethany shrieked.

Sam had now caught up with them. 'What's going on?' he demanded.

'Catriona's inside the house,' Bethany panted, running out of breath.

Sam turned to Johnny. 'Are you mad?'

'Hey,' Johnny protested, 'lighten up.'

'Have you totally lost it?'

'Watch your language,' Johnny retaliated. 'I was the one who alerted the emergency services, remember?'

'Stop it, you two.' Bethany tried to separate the pair of them, as they looked ready to square up for a fight.

Johnny shook Sam's hands off his shoulders. 'Here, I grabbed a couple of Wendel's torches. I found them by the back door. We'll need them to see where we're going.'

'No one else is going inside.' Sam snatched up one of the flashlights.

'We need to go after Catriona.' Bethany's breath came in loud sobs.

'It was the costumes,' Johnny began to explain.

'What costumes?' Sam shouted.

'Merrill was using one of the bedrooms as a store room.' Bethany's chest hurt, she was talking so quickly. 'But never mind all that now.'

'And you let Catriona go inside on her own?' Bethany had never seen Sam so angry. 'The whole place could go up in flames any minute.'

'I didn't *let* her; she did her own thing. I expect she thought she'd try to save what she could. She's a plucky girl.'

'She's a fool.'

'Don't you dare speak about her like that,' Johnny spluttered.

'What are you doing?' Bethany tugged at Sam's leather jacket.

'I'm going in.'

'No.' Bethany pulled harder, but Sam was stronger than her. 'You said no one was to go in.'

'I don't have any choice.'

'I'm coming with you,' Johnny shouted, unceremoniously shoving Bethany to one side.

'Stay where you are, both of you.' Sam began running towards the conservatory. 'Johnny, look after Bethany.'

'Go after him,' Bethany bellowed at Johnny, shouting to make her voice heard above the wailing of sirens.

'Sam said I was to look after you.'

'If you won't go after him, I will.'

Johnny leapt forward and grabbed Bethany's arm.

'Let go of me,' she shrieked.

'You heard him. Neither of us is going in.'

'Sam's in there.'

'So is Catriona, but it won't do any good us adding to the confusion.'

'Some of the upstairs rooms aren't safe.'

'All the more reason to stay put.'

'Is there anyone inside?' A helmeted fire officer barked the question at them as he strode down the path.

'My girlfriend.' Johnny released his hold on Bethany's arm.

'What's her name?'

'Catriona.'

'Anyone else?'

'Mr Richards. He's a friend,' Johnny added. 'He's gone inside too.'

'Who are you?' the fire officer enquired.

'Johnny Morton. I was the one who called you.'

'And you?'

'Bethany Burnett. It's my godfather's house,' she spluttered still not able to breathe freely.

'You're sure there's no one else inside?'

'Absolutely.'

'Then please stand out of the way and make sure no one else attempts any heroics.'

The tone of the fireman indicated exactly what he thought of interfering members of the public. Bethany opened her mouth to protest but received a sharp nudge in the ribs from Johnny.

'Do as he says. We don't want to get ourselves arrested.'

'There has to be some way we can help.'

'Like what?'

'I don't know. Shouldn't I be on the premises for insurance purposes?'

'Not if the building's on fire. Let's get out of the way like the man said.' Johnny began to hustle her towards a quieter part of the lawn. 'Where are your shoes?'

'I've no idea.'

'Wait here.'

Ducking to avoid being spotted by the fire fighters Johnny zigzagged down to the conservatory. He was back a moment later, clutching a pair of boots. 'Here,' he said, 'put these on.'

Bethany rammed her feet into the too-big boots.

'I've brought you a jacket too.'

Behind them they could hear the hose being unfurled and instructions being shouted.

'What were you doing here, anyway?' Bethany wiped a muddy hand across her face, trying to ignore the crackling of splintering wood beams.

'Trying to avoid Harland Somerville. That was the plan until we spotted flames at an upstairs window. After that I'm not too sure what happened.'

With calm efficiency, the fire crew trained their hoses on the outside walls of the house, killing the flames leaping from an upstairs window.

Bethany waved her torch towards the

upper floor of the house. 'Can you see anything?'

'There,' Johnny shouted. 'Isn't that Catriona?' A figure staggered out through the conservatory door.

'Over here!' Bethany signalled with her torch.

Catriona began running towards them, tripping over armfuls of costumes. 'I saved what I could,' she began to explain before Johnny enveloped her in his arms and kissed her with such intensity Bethany was forced to look away. 'Don't ever do anything like that again,' he sobbed against her hair.

Bethany flashed her torch at the house and caught sight of Sam strolling across the grass, clutching some wigs. 'I've been given an earful by one of the firemen,' he protested.

'You deserved it.' Bethany could hardly disguise her relief. 'What made you barge in like that? Why didn't you let me come in with you?'

'It may have escaped your notice, but our leading lady was inside a burning building, and no way were you coming in with me.'

Bethany began coughing as the wind changed direction and blew a wave of smoke at them. 'It would've served you right if the ceiling had collapsed on you.'

'For a moment there I thought you might've been worried about me.' Sam gave a rueful smile.

Bethany's eyes were now streaming from the smell of dampened-down ashes. 'It's no joking matter.'

'Sorry.' Sam looked suitably contrite. 'As it turned out, my heroics were unnecessary. I bumped into Catriona making her way downstairs with half the contents of Richards Productions wardrobe department.'

'Any idea what caused the fire?' Johnny, still with his arm around Catriona, interrupted him.

'The electrics?' Sam suggested. 'They always were suspect. It would only have needed one spark to set things off.'

'There was a sort of scorched

electrical smell,' Catriona admitted. 'At least I think there was. It was difficult to tell with all that was going on.'

'The hangings around the beds are so old they're ridden with moths,' Bethany agreed.

'You're not suggesting the moths started it?'

Catriona had no right to look so calm, Bethany thought, as the girl smiled sweetly at her. She was the only one amongst them who didn't resemble a scarecrow and smell of decaying leaves, yet she had been the one who regardless of her own safety had rushed into a burning house.

'I'm not suggesting anything of the sort.' Bethany was forced to smile back. 'You're sure you're OK?' she asked.

'Never felt better.' A dimple dented Catriona's cheek. 'I like playing the heroine. Pity there's no chance of an Oscar.'

Now that everyone was safe, Bethany allowed herself to relax a little. 'I'm sure Sam will forget to say it, Catriona, but thanks for saving the day.'

'Whatever. You're safe, and that's all that matters.' Johnny crushed Catriona to his chest again.

'I'm glad we've all come out of that one unscathed,' Sam murmured in Bethany's ear.

She knew she should have been repelled by Sam's appearance. His face was smudged and he smelt strongly of smoke. Instead, she wanted him to clasp her in his arms the same way Johnny was comforting Catriona. She contented herself with saying, 'If and when Wendel reappears, he's going to get such a rocket. He could've put everyone's lives in danger.'

'He couldn't possibly have known there'd be a fire,' Sam said.

'I hope the press don't get hold of this one,' Johnny voiced a new fear. 'If they learn of Catriona's heroics, there'll be no stopping them.'

'I doubt we'll be able to keep something like this quiet,' Sam said.

'Harland knows about the fire,'

Bethany remembered. 'He was with me when your call came through, Johnny.'

'And if no one else does, he'll alert the media.'

Catriona looked at Sam. 'What do you suggest we do?'

'Make ourselves scarce before someone recognises you?'

'And the costumes?' Catriona was still clutching her haul. 'We can't dump them on the grass.'

'There's the old summerhouse,' Bethany suggested. 'It's not up to much, but not many people know of its existence. It's dry and hidden away from sight.'

'Then let's get going,' Sam said.

'Here, Catriona,' said Johnny, 'stick one of these wigs on your head as a disguise.'

'Look out,' Sam warned in an urgent voice as the sound of raised voices reached their ears. 'Isn't that Harland Somerville?'

'And he's got a photographer with him,' Bethany added.

'And they're heading this way.'

Johnny grimaced.

'Quick,' Bethany said, grabbing Sam's hand, 'round the back. I know a short cut.'

'Make sure you don't drape the dresses in the mud,' Catriona pleaded.

'Who cares about the dresses? Get a move on,' Johnny urged as they raced across the lawn.

Squashed in the confines of the old summerhouse, Sam made a space for Catriona on the rickety wooden bench while Johnny and Bethany occupied a couple of ancient deckchairs.

'I hope this thing is safe.' Johnny wriggled his lanky frame into a more comfortable position.

There was a loud crash as Catriona collided with a watering can and burst into gales of laughter. 'When I come to write my memoirs,' she announced, 'this is definitely one for the record books.'

'Thank heavens no one's taking pictures.' Johnny continued to wriggle about in his deckchair. 'My image would never survive the fallout.'

'Come on, Bethany,' Catriona ordered her, 'I'm pulling rank. Sit next to Sam and don't argue.'

'Good idea,' Johnny agreed. 'Up you go, Bethany.'

Before she could protest, Johnny manhandled her out of her deckchair and into the space next to Sam.

'Why don't we follow their example?' Sam's voice was warm against Bethany's ear.

Johnny and Catriona, with their arms entwined around each other, appeared to be taking up where they'd earlier left off.

'And do what?' Bethany's heartbeat began to dance the tango.

'We need some comfort therapy. We've all had a nasty shock.'

'I'm fine, really,' Bethany insisted.

'I don't think so,' Sam contradicted her.

The smell of dead smoke permeating the confines of the summerhouse was overpowering; and along with the aroma of dank wood, Bethany was finding it difficult to breathe. 'What exactly did you have in mind?' Her voice came out as a husky croak.

'This,' Sam said.

As he lowered his lips to hers, there was a blinding flash.

15

'Park House has agreed to double as Waterbridge Manor for the final few takes,' Sam informed Bethany. Yet again they were seated in the snug of The Goose and Galleon. 'I've given instructions to the cast and crew to prepare to relocate.' He raised his voice against a background of shouted commands as scenery and costumes were loaded onto a container lorry. 'With clever camera angles and blurred focuses, it should work. We'll be doing the outside shots in their water garden. It's a highlighted feature of the property and totally in keeping with the period.'

'Then Waterbridge has had its day?' Bethany had expected as much but hadn't expected to feel quite so disappointed. 'Even though the damage isn't as bad as everyone expected?'

''Fraid so,' Sam said with a look of

regret. 'There's no way the insurance can be renewed; and even if by the remotest chance there was, it'd take an age to sort things out. We don't have the time, and time is money in this business.'

Bethany nodded. 'And you did come back for the money, didn't you?'

It was an unkind remark, and the moment she spoke Bethany felt ashamed for being so ungrateful. Everyone, including Sam, had helped out in the aftermath of the fire and they deserved her gratitude, not nasty comments.

'Sorry,' she mumbled, looking down at the carpet. 'That was uncalled for.'

What Sam said made sense. Three days after the incident, the rooms still reeked of smoke, the upper floors had been rendered unsafe, and the ceilings had been deemed too fragile to withstand any pressure.

Bethany had been allowed back into the property, accompanied by a qualified assessor as he did his rounds to inspect the extent of the damage, but everyone else had been banned from entering the manor.

'You've been through a lot,' Sam sympathised. 'Anyone else would've buckled under the pressure.'

His kindness only made Bethany feel worse. 'I can't help feeling Wendel will hold me responsible.'

'No way.' Sam's eyebrows drew together in an angry frown.

'I was the one who gave permission for the costumes to be stored in the house.'

'If anyone's going to be accused of irresponsibility, it has to be Wendel. I know he's your godfather, and I don't like to speak ill of him, but he did rather land you in it, taking off like that without a word to anybody.'

'Now you're getting the hang of Wendel.' Bethany smiled.

Sam fixed her with a suspicious look. 'If I didn't know better, I'd say you were laughing at me.'

'Not laughing, merely agreeing with you.'

'Whatever.' Sam looked unconvinced.

'We've a lot to thank Johnny Morton for. And Catriona,' he added.

'I'm so glad she didn't go difficult on you.'

'Things could've been very different if she had,' Sam agreed. 'That's why I'm so anxious to keep to schedule. Her diary is fully booked months ahead, and we can't afford to overrun.'

'You don't intend to go difficult on Wendel, do you?' Bethany enquired.

'If you mean will he be hearing from my legal people, I can't say anything at this stage. If the decision were in my hands, then it'd be a definite no, but I don't have the final word.'

'What about Leo Somerville? Does he know what's happened?' Bethany asked after a pause.

'Harland tells me he's been in touch.'

'The hero of the hour,' Bethany acknowledged with another wry smile. Harland had made headlines the day following the fire. His photo was on the front of all the news-sheets as he recounted his story of how he had raced into the flames without a thought for his own personal safety to rescue the family pets, not realising they had been relocated. The house had not been a raging inferno, but mention of animals in distress ensured Harland's story was front-page news.

'I'm prepared to let him have his moment of glory if it keeps everyone else out of trouble,' Sam agreed.

'Who would've thought he had it in him to dash into a burning house to save a terrier and a pregnant rabbit?'

'Whilst we cowered away in the summerhouse?' Sam's eyes danced with amusement.

'Not our finest hour,' Bethany agreed. 'I still don't know how that weasel of a photographer found us.'

She could still remember her shock as the summerhouse door burst open and a flashbulb went off in her face. They had been crushed together on the wobbly wooden bench, and Sam had been holding her hand and about to kiss her.

'He was probably the same one who took that photo of you and Anthony playing snowballs. Apparently he'd been hanging around for days.'

'Thank goodness Catriona had the sense to stick one of the wigs on her head and pretend to be Merrill's wardrobe assistant.'

'I don't know how I kept my face straight.' Sam laughed. 'But the weasel didn't recognise her, so I think we got away with it.'

Johnny and Catriona had managed to slip away unnoticed while Harland was holding forth on the front lawn. Sam and Bethany had hung around for a while until the house was secured and pronounced safe from further fire damage, then they'd followed Johnny and Catriona's example and headed back to The Goose and Galleon for a night of anxious enquiries and endless interviews.

'Has Anthony been in touch with you?' Bethany asked.

'He'll be back on set on schedule as soon as we relocate. And as he's now the proud father of a second daughter, the publicity department plans to make a major announcement once the fuss over the fire has died down. Catriona's prepared to admit their relationship was a bluff to hide what was actually going on in Anthony's personal life. It's the stuff of gossip mags.' A look of distaste crossed Sam's face. 'But all this advance publicity should ensure that *Love Will Find a Way* will be the hit of the year. In Harland-speak, we are hot.'

'You don't sound very enthusiastic about the prospect of having a hit on your hands.'

'It's not a side of the business I enjoy,' Sam admitted. 'The interviews, answering the same endless questions, appearing on chat shows . . . '

Bethany longed to ask if his aversion to the media was anything to do with his much-publicised prolonged disappearance, but she recognised that to do so would be a step too far. Outside she heard a container lorry start up and drive out of the forecourt.

'About Park House,' Sam began tentatively, 'there's something I have to tell you.'

'There's no job for me in the new set-up, is there?'

'I'm sure we could find you something.'

'You don't have to,' Bethany insisted. 'I knew this was only a temporary position.'

'One you took under extreme pressure, if I recall.'

Bethany refused to rise to Sam's bait.

'Anyway,' he continued when she didn't respond, 'Park House has its own team of dedicated staff, and under the terms of the new insurance we have to employ them.'

'I understand. It's time I got my life sorted out. It's been on hold since I returned from Canada.'

'Would you . . . ' Sam paused. ' . . . think about going abroad again?'

'You mean to Canada?'

'I was thinking more of an under-developed country.'

'It's not a part of the world I've ever visited.'

'Would you be interested — ' Sam

leaned forward, the light of enthusiasm back in his eyes. ' — in a position in the third world?'

'I'd need to give it some consideration.'

'Naturally. But in theory?'

Bethany paused, her suspicions aroused. 'If it's anything of a financial nature involving Leo Somerville, then the answer is no.'

A fleeting expression of disappointment crossed Sam's face. 'Is that your last word on the matter?'

'Yes.'

'You wouldn't reconsider?'

'Absolutely not.'

'Are you sure I can't change your mind?'

'More than sure.'

'In that case, I'd best be off.' Sam finished his coffee.

'You're going now?' Bethany hadn't expected his departure to be quite so sudden.

'I am.' He held out his hand. 'Until we meet again.'

'That sounds very final.'

'For the moment it has to be.'

The touch of his hand against hers was an impersonal gesture. Their relationship was at an end. Sam was too involved with Leo Somerville for Bethany to consider any proposition he had to offer, but her decision left her feeling flat and unmotivated.

She stood at the window and watched Sam drive out of the car park with a sinking heart. More cars followed him soon, leaving only Wendel's bike leaning against the fence. No doubt he would eventually reclaim it.

'Still here?' Harland lounged in the doorway.

'I could say the same thing about you.' Bethany turned to face him.

'What's it like to be out of a job again?' he taunted her with an unpleasant smile.

The only way to deal with Harland was to stand up to him, something Bethany had discovered to her cost. 'You tell me.'

'I have a job,' Harland blustered. 'I'm keeping an eye on things for my uncle.'

'I'm sure you are.'

'I report back to him on a daily basis.'

'It was you who told him all about the fire?'

'He was impressed with the way I handled the publicity.' Harland looked inordinately pleased with himself.

'Yes, you did very well.' Bethany was beginning to grow bored with agreeing with everything he said.

Harland looked in no hurry to move 'By the way, did you ever get the chance to ask Sam about The Dragon?'

'I've had other things on my mind.'

'I wondered, because I thought I heard him mention the underdeveloped world.'

'Why does The Dragon matter so much to you?' Bethany asked, her curiosity piqued.

'I thought you ought to know the sort of man Sam is before you start falling in love with him.'

'I'm not falling in love with him, and that's the most ridiculous remark I've ever heard you make.' Bethany's face flamed with a mixture of embarrassment and anger.

'Have I touched a raw nerve?' Harland taunted.

'Now you're being absurd.'

'Good, because Sam won't stand by you if things should go pear-shaped.'

'You mean I'll get the blame for something I didn't do? Well don't worry, I've had experience of that sort of thing. I'm sure I'll be able to pick myself up off the floor. I've done it before.'

Harland flushed. 'What's past is past.'

'Again, I so totally agree with you.'

'I'd like us to be friends.' Harland moved away from the doorway and into the room, an ingratiating smile on his face. 'That business with Catriona,' he said, adopting a laid-back stance, 'it was nothing, really. Surely you're not jealous of her?'

'Please excuse me.' Bethany made to move past him. She didn't trust herself not to inflict a physical injury on him. He was conceited beyond belief.

'Where are you going?'

'Up to Waterbridge Manor.'

'That burnt-out old heap? There's nothing for you there.'

Although Harland was goading her, his words were not that far from the truth. The manor would require a lot of work and money to be restored to its former state. Money that Wendel did not have.

'Thank you so much for all you did,' she said with a sweet smile, 'and for informing the press that I was hiding in the summerhouse.' Bethany could tell by the expression on Harland's face that her jibe had hit home.

'I don't know what you're talking about,' he blustered.

'As usual, Harland, you were protecting your own back, something you're very good at. Now if there's nothing else?'

Harland's eyes narrowed. 'You haven't heard the last of this.'

'I daresay. But you know what, Harland? I don't care. You no longer have the power to affect my life.'

'We'll see about that.' His words rang in her ears as she closed the door behind her.

'It's not his lucky day, is it?' a voice greeted her in the corridor.

'Catriona?' Bethany stepped back in surprise. 'I thought you'd already left.'

'I'm waiting for Johnny.'

'I shouldn't hang around if I were you unless you want to bump into Harland.'

Catriona was unable to contain her amusement as her face lit up with barely suppressed laughter. 'I already have.'

'And?' Bethany could tell from the expression on Catriona's face that there was more to come.

'Guess what?'

'I couldn't possibly.'

'I told him he was a worm who should think about getting a life of his own and not live on the reflected glory of his uncle.'

'You didn't!' Bethany sagged against the wall in surprise.

'Somebody had to say it.'

'I agree, but was that a wise move?'

'I don't like the way he treats everyone, so I thought blow it, it's time for a few home truths.'

'How did he take it?'

'Not well. It's probably why he came on to you to prove he still had the magic touch. Sorry,' Catriona apologised, 'that came out badly.'

'Don't worry,' Bethany assured her. 'I know exactly what you mean.'

'That sounds like Johnny arriving.' Catriona peered through the door as a saloon car eased into the forecourt.

Bethany looked over her shoulder. 'If it is, then his fortune has definitely gone up in the world. That car is top of the range.'

'You're right. It isn't Johnny.' Catriona frowned as a uniformed chauffeur descended from the car and opened the rear passenger door. A white-haired man got out and glanced across the fore-court. 'Do you recognise him?'

'I do,' Bethany said with a sinking heart. 'It's Leo Somerville.'

16

'You're not serious?' Catriona's huge dark eyes reflected her anxiety.

'I was never more serious in my life,' Bethany replied, feeling equally as anxious.

'You don't think he's come about me and Johnny, do you? Harland's probably told him everything.'

'Or his version of everything,' Bethany corrected her.

'In that case I won't come out of it well, will I?'

'You've no need to worry.'

'How can you be sure?'

'I hate to say this, but Leo Somerville is a fair man.'

'I don't think I want to speak to him,' Catriona said.

'I'm not too keen on the idea either. I expect he's come about the fire or to issue Wendel with a writ.'

Catriona was all smiles again. 'Leo can't blame you or Wendel for the fire.'

'He'll probably have a good go.'

'You said he was a fair man.'

Bethany tossed back her head. 'What say we face him together?' she suggested. 'I could do with some support.'

'Sisters under the skin?' Catriona suggested with a tentative smile.

'Exactly.'

The girls slapped palms, then waited as heavy footsteps made their way across the car park.

'Ladies,' Leo Somerville greeted them from the doorway with a courteous smile. 'Lovely to see you. Shall we make our way to the snug?'

Both women were left with the impression that refusal was not an option. The snug seemed to shrink in Leo Somerville's presence. He was a big man in every meaning of the word.

'I hope you're both well,' he said.

'Yes, thank you,' Bethany replied, determined to keep things as polite as possible.

'Would you like to speak to Harland?' Catriona offered. 'He's around somewhere.'

'It's actually Miss Burnett I've come to talk to.'

Bethany's newfound confidence rapidly deserted her.

'I see,' Catriona said in a faint voice, casting Bethany a sympathetic glance, then straightening her shoulders she stood square in front of Leo. 'You don't mind if I stay, do you?'

'What I have to say to Miss Burnett is of a private nature.'

'I understand, and I know your private affairs are none of my business, but I want to say that Bethany has been brilliant on set. Sam thinks so too.'

Bethany was unable to contain a blush. Catriona was being outrageous. Sam thought nothing of the sort.

'She's kind and considerate,' Catriona battled on, not in the least discomfited by her economy with the truth, 'and has done all sorts of things that strictly speaking were not part of her official duties

— like covering up for Anthony, and taking the pressure off Sam by shielding him from nuisance calls.'

'I know; I was on the receiving end of one of her terse telephone dismissals,' Leo said with a wry smile, then turned to face Bethany. 'By the way, Sam never did get back to me, and you promised he would.'

'I . . . ' Bethany's mouth dried up. 'Sorry,' was all she could manage.

'Never mind that.' Catriona dismissed Leo's interruption with a wave of her hand. 'I haven't finished.'

'Forgive me,' Leo apologised. 'I thought you had. Please continue.'

'Bethany very sweetly arranged for Bouncer and Furry to be farmed out because I have an allergy to animal fur. Actually, Furry — that's the rabbit started off as a male, but when she fell pregnant everyone realised we'd made a huge mistake.' Catriona giggled.

Bethany longed to tell her to shut up but she didn't have the heart. The lovely girl was doing her best to make a case for Bethany, but from the expression on Leo's face she suspected Catriona was only making things worse.

'And whatever your wretched nephew told you,' Catriona ploughed on, 'we weren't hiding in the summerhouse — we were protecting some very expensive costumes and the wigs.'

'It was actually Catriona and Sam who plunged into the raging inferno,' Bethany couldn't resist pointing out, 'not Harland. He turned up later. I mean, he might've plunged into the conservatory, but we didn't see it.' It was Bethany who now ground to a halt. Between them, she and Catriona were not doing well.

'So there.' Catriona took over the reins again, crossing her arms in challenge. 'And don't you dare start accusing Bethany of starting the fire.'

'I wouldn't dream of it,' was Leo's mild response.

'What on earth is going on in here?' Johnny poked his head round the door. 'Who are you?' He glared at Leo.

'I, young man, am Leo Somerville. Who are you?'

Johnny paled under the older man's scrutiny. 'Leo Somerville?' he echoed in a faint voice, adding, 'Are you sure?'

Bethany raised her eyebrows in despair. Didn't the pair of them realise who they were talking to? Leo Somerville held their future in his hands and they were treating him like a nobody.

'This is Johnny Morton,' Catriona announced with a proud smile. 'He's a brilliant cameraman.'

Leo held up a hand. 'Thank you, Ms Cleeve. I don't doubt Sam's whole team is very professional.'

'I have another confession,' Catriona battled on.

'Is now the right time?' Leo asked.

'In case you thought I was in a relationship with Harland, I'm not. But since working with Johnny, I've come to value his professionalism, and we get on very well together.' Catriona finally ground to a halt.

The tips of Johnny's ears turned pink

with embarrassment. 'Maybe Mr Somerville is right, Catriona,' he said. 'Our relationship is something we can discuss later.'

'Thank you, Mr Morton. Now as I understand it, filming has been rescheduled?'

'Yes, that's right, sir.'

'Then may I suggest you escort Ms Cleeve to Park House and leave the situation here to me?'

'Not if you're going to have a go at Bethany.' Johnny now stood his ground.

Bethany clenched her fists in frustration. Why didn't Johnny get out while the going was good? You could only push Leo Somerville so far, and to Bethany it looked as though they were overdrawn.

'It wasn't Bethany's fault Waterbridge Manor caught fire. It was the wiring — at least, I think it was. Nothing's been confirmed yet, but we had lots of power cuts and stuff.'

'So I've been given to understand. But you needn't worry; I promise not to have a go at Miss Burnett, as you so eloquently put it. And if things should get heated, I understand not all the crew have left, so why don't you put the word round to those who are still here that I'm with Miss Burnett in the snug? And if my emotions should get the better of me, they're free to intervene.'

Catriona and Johnny stared at each other, unsure what to do.

'Go on,' Bethany urged them. 'Mr Somerville is a man of his word. I give you my guarantee he'll behave like a gentleman.'

'Thank you.' Leo nodded in her direction.

'If you're sure?' Johnny hesitated.

'Off you go,' Bethany insisted.

Catriona embraced her. 'You will keep in touch, won't you?'

'I promise.'

'We'll ring you tonight,' Johnny promised.

'May I sit down?' Leo asked after they had left. 'My hip is being troublesome but I hate to give in to these things.'

It was then Bethany noticed he was leaning heavily on a stick. 'Of course. I'm so sorry. Is there anything I can get you?'

'Thank you, but no, unless you happen to have a new hip on you?' He smiled.

'I'm afraid I can't oblige.'

'At last I seem to have found something you can't do.'

Bethany followed Leo's example and sat down. It felt strange to be sitting in The Goose and Galleon opposite the man who had irrevocably changed her life.

'I come here in the spirit of friendship,' he explained.

'You do?'

'And I don't know where to start.'

'To save you any embarrassment, I have no intention of going to Park House with the crew. Sam's explained the situation,' Bethany informed him, 'so you have no need to dismiss me a second time. I've already been let go.'

'I had no reason to dismiss you the

first time, but I did so because I knew you weren't involved in Harland's financial schemes.'

His words almost robbed Bethany of the power of speech. 'If you knew I was innocent of any wrongdoing, why didn't you support me?'

'Because I wanted you out of Harland's life. It suited my plans. And if that sounds harsh, then I truly am sorry, but it was the only action I could take. Harland's my nephew and nothing can change that, but I hope I know right from wrong. He has his weaknesses and I can control them, but I didn't want him ruining your life, so I stepped in before he went too far and before the authorities could take things further.'

Bethany slumped against the back of her chair, then straightened up. Slumping was negative body language, and she didn't want Leo Somerville picking up on it. 'I'm not sure I understand any of that, but it sounds as though you acted with the best of interests.'

'That was my intention. I would've done more for you, but you went off to Canada, and frankly I thought being with your family was the safest place for you. But I decided that if the chance presented itself for me to help you out in any way, then I would do what I could. So I recommended Waterbridge Manor to Sam Richards.'

'Why?'

'I knew Wendel was your godfather and that you're very close. I guessed that you'd visit him when you came home. I thought it would be a perfect opportunity for you to meet Sam.'

'Why did you want me to meet Sam?' Bethany was becoming more confused by the minute. 'And why are you taking such a great interest in my life?'

'When I was setting out early in my career, I was given a break by a powerful man. I came from a humble background, and without his help I probably wouldn't be where I am today. I've always vowed to act in the same manner if I could.'

'Are you saying you want to give me a break?'

'I know I'll have my hands full persuading you I'm on the level, but yes, that's the general thrust.'

'Why me?' Bethany repeated her question.

'You're a person I can trust, and I think you and Sam Richards would make a good team.'

'Doing what?'

They both jumped as the door to the snug was flung open and Harland crashed into the room. 'Uncle Leo.' He hugged the older man. 'I didn't know you were here. Nobody told me.'

Leo Somerville returned his nephew's greeting, moving his stick away from Harland's enthusiastic embrace. 'Have you come to inspect the fire damage?'

'That situation is now out of my hands,' Leo replied calmly, 'but I heard all about your exploits.'

Bethany's eyes widened in surprise. Leo Somerville had actually winked at her.

'You saw me on the news?' Harland was visibly preening.

'I did indeed. Now, I understand you were on your way somewhere? Please don't let me detain you.'

'I can always stay on.' Harland cast a suspicious glance in Bethany's direction. 'We've lots to talk about.'

'Why don't you join the others at Park House?' Leo suggested.

'What about Bethany?' Harland asked uncertainly.

'You needn't concern yourself with Bethany.'

'I can drive you over to Park House now if your hip's painful.'

'Thank you for the offer, but I can manage.'

Leo showed no signs of moving, and Harland began to look less sure of his situation. 'Will you be over later?' he asked.'

'I will indeed.'

'If you're sure there's nothing I can do?' Harland still portrayed a marked reluctance to leave.

'I'd like you to check up on things for me there. Keep an eye on what's happening and report back.'

'Of course,' Harland agreed. Bethany admired Leo's tactics. There was nothing Harland liked better than interfering. 'By the way,' he added, 'I overheard Sam Richards telling Bethany that there was no job for her in the new set-up.'

'Is that so?'

'Park House has its own highly trained staff.'

'Indeed it does.'

'I can't see their bedrooms catching fire.'

'That's a good thing to know.'

Harland shuffled his feet. 'I'll be off then. I guess this is goodbye, Bethany, now your services are no longer required.' It seemed he could not resist a final taunt.

'Goodbye, Harland.' Bethany did her best to keep her voice pleasant. 'And good luck.'

'Thank you for that,' Leo said after Harland had gone.

'For what?'

'Not saying what you really wanted to say. It takes practice holding your tongue with Harland, but one gets the hang of it eventually. Now where were we?'

'Mr Somerville.'

'I think we can dispense with the formalities. It's Leo, Bethany,' he said.

'Very well. Leo.' She took a deep breath. 'I don't know what you've got in mind regarding my future.'

'Then let me enlighten you.'

'I want to say,' Bethany continued, 'before you go any further, that I don't need your help. I appreciate your motives, but I prefer to make my own way in life.'

'I thought you'd say that.'

'Then you'll forgive me for saying you haven't been disappointed.'

'Have you heard of The Dragon?'

Bethany stiffened. 'Harland has mentioned it.'

'My nephew only knows what I choose to tell him, and I blush to admit my description of its activities wasn't entirely one hundred percent accurate.'

'I don't follow you.'

'It suits me to let Harland think it's a financial arrangement with an under-developed country. I couched my description in terms Harland would understand. I also allowed him to host a champagne fundraiser at a luxury hotel. Harland is a sociable person and I was playing to his strengths.'

'Is it another scam?'

Leo held up a hand. 'That's a term I don't use. I have never, nor do I ever, intend to be involved in a scam.'

'That was rude of me. I apologise.'

'It was an understandable reaction, given the circumstances.'

'Is The Dragon a charity?' Bethany asked.

'It's a foundation.'

'Does The Dragon have anything to do with Sam's unexplained disappear-ance two years ago?'

'It does,' Leo admitted, 'in a roundabout way.'

'Darling,' a voice interrupted them as yet again the door to the snug was opened with formidable force, 'we're so sorry. Can you ever forgive us?'

The next moment Bethany was enveloped in a bear-crushing hug. She sneezed as the fake fur collar of Lottie's coat tickled her nostrils.

'Whatever must you think of us? My poor baby, you were so brave, fighting back the flames all on your own.'

'Lottie, I can't breathe.' Bethany wriggled in her embrace.

Lottie released her and held her at arm's length. 'Thank goodness you weren't burnt to death. I shudder to think what could've happened.'

'Nothing did happen, Lottie, and I'm absolutely fine,' Bethany assured her.

'We should've been here for you and we weren't. I don't know how we can ever make it up to you, but I'll do my best, I promise.'

Bethany glanced over Lottie's shoulder to where Wendel was fixed in the doorway.

'Hello, Angel,' he greeted her. 'Am I forgiven? If I am, can I have a hug too?'

17

'Miss St James, it's good to see you again,' Leo Somerville greeted her with a courteous nod of his head.

'Hello, Leo, you old rogue. I hope you haven't been bullying Bethany, because if you have you'll have me to deal with.'

'I'm afraid you'll have to take your place in the queue. May I offer you my belated congratulations?'

'You may, and less of the 'Miss St James'. It's Lottie.'

'Well, Lottie, I don't need to tell you that you've caused a lot of trouble, do I?'

'Story of my life,' Lottie admitted with a rueful smile. 'Still, all that's about to change.'

'Wendel.' Bethany hugged her god-father. 'You are the most impossible person. I don't know why I should ever speak to you again.'

'Then I'm forgiven?' He smiled.

'Why did you have to run away and not tell anyone where you were going or what you were up to? You're hardly a teenager.'

'At the risk of sounding ungallant, that was Lottie's idea. I told you she was a drama queen. I had to indulge her, didn't I? I think she had some idea that I'd run out on her again if she didn't look sharp.'

'You let everybody down,' Bethany chided him.

'Don't I always?'

'Yes,' Bethany acknowledged.

'I did try to tell you our plans, but we were interrupted, if you recall, by that wretched rabbit.'

'Promise me you'll never do it again.'

'I promise I have absolutely no intention of running off to get married again. For a start, Lottie wouldn't allow it.' He cast an affectionate glance over to where his new wife was engaged in a spirited conversation with Leo.

'That's not what I meant and you know it.'

'Scout's honour, no more disappearing without telling you where I'm going. Will that do?'

'I suppose that is all I'm going to get.'

'You know,' Wendel confided, 'Lottie's never been married before, and she loves being Mrs Wendel Nelson.'

Wendel looked so happy it was impossible for Bethany to remain cross with him. 'Then I wish the both of you every happiness.'

'What do you think of my ring?' Lottie flashed a solitaire diamond under Bethany's nose.

Leo frowned. 'It's not a very big one.'

'That surprised you, didn't it?' Lottie laughed. 'I didn't want a huge great movie-star rock thing. This little ring is absolutely perfect.' She linked arms with Wendel. 'As is my new husband.'

'Steady on, Lottie.' Wendel's voice sounded decidedly gruff. 'Don't go all soppy on me.'

'I've waited long enough for this day,

so you're not doing me out of showing the boys and girls my ring. By the way, it's very quiet. Where is everybody?'

'In the throes of moving over to Park House,' Leo replied. 'In case you hadn't heard, there was a fire at Waterbridge Manor.'

Lottie ignored the jibe and linked her other arm through Bethany's. 'Old Sir Anthony came up with the goods, did he? What do you think of my new family, Leo?'

'I think you're an extremely lucky lady, Lottie.'

'So do I, and now that I'm a respectable married lady, I intend to retire from acting,' she announced.

'Won't you find life dull?' Leo asked.

'I may take the occasional cameo role to keep my hand in, but Wendel and I have decided we'll do up Waterbridge Manor, then rent the rooms out as holiday lets. I shall play the grand hostess. It's going to be the most tremendous fun.'

'It'll also be a lot of hard work.' Leo

sounded unimpressed by her plans.

'And where will you live?' Bethany asked. 'The manor's not really habitable.'

'I don't know. Probably in a mobile home in the grounds.'

Leo made a choking noise at the back of his throat. 'That I've got to see.'

'I'll have you know I grew up in a caravan,' Lottie said.

'They've changed a lot since then,' Leo pointed out.

'I expect it'll all come back to me. You can't dent my enthusiasm, Leo Somerville, so don't even try.'

'No need to look so worried, Angel,' Wendel said to Bethany. 'Lottie's a shrewd old thing. You wouldn't believe it, but underneath that scatty exterior lurks a brain as sharp as any businessman's. Over the years she's made some wise investments, and she now wants to move into property, so where better to start than the manor?'

'Is working hard for a living your sort of thing?' Bethany enquired, remembering how Mary used to have to pay all their bills and deal with the tradesmen.

'With Lottie by my side, how can I go wrong? Isn't she marvellous?'

'She's certainly something else,' Bethany agreed.

'I think,' Lottie announced, 'that you and I, Leo, should entertain each other and leave Wendel and Bethany to play catch-up.'

Leo did not look enthralled by the prospect of entertaining Lottie for the afternoon. 'I haven't finished talking to Bethany.'

'There's plenty of time for all that later,' Lottie said. 'Tell you what — your driver can take us over to Park House now. I can show everyone my ring, then when we've finished up there it will be time for dinner. We can all go out and celebrate. Does that sound like a plan?'

Leo cast an uncertain glance in Bethany's direction. 'I suppose whatever I have to say can keep.'

'That's the spirit. Goodbye, darlings.' She gave Wendel an airy wave and kissed Bethany on the cheek. 'There's no one in this world I'd rather have for a goddaughter, although I know technically I'm not really your godmother.'

'You can be an honorary one,' Bethany said.

'Thank you, darling. Now I've taken Wendel off your hands, you can get on with your life — and don't let that divine Sam Richards slip through your fingers.'

Bethany stiffened. 'Lottie, don't interfere,' Wendel chided her.

'Why shouldn't I?' Lottie didn't look in the least abashed. 'They'd make a wonderful team. Leo and I will be back later, so get all you've got to say to each other out of the way. Bye.' She blew them a kiss.

'Would you like to go out too?' Wendel asked when things had settled down after Lottie's departure with Leo.

Bethany drew her thoughts back to the present. 'Not unless you want to see Waterbridge Manor.'

Wendel shook his head. 'I presume the old girl is still standing?'

'She is, if a little battle-scarred.'

'Then let's stay here.' Wendel settled in the seat Leo had recently vacated. 'What shall we talk about?'

'I should update you on everything that's been happening here.'

'I'll find out soon enough.' Wendel paused. 'Tell me to mind my own business if you like, Angel,' he began, 'but I can tell when something's worrying you, and I don't think it's got anything to do with my escapades. Has Lottie hit the nail on the head about you and Sam? Is there anything I should know?'

'Have you heard of The Dragon?' Bethany asked.

'I can't say I have.'

'Leo was going to tell me all about it.'

'Before Lottie and I burst in?' Wendel made a rueful face. 'I'm sorry about that. All I can say is I noticed the dragonhead pin that Sam used to wear in the lapel of that biker jacket of his, and he had a similar logo on his T-shirt. I wondered about its significance at the time.'

'Lottie's never mentioned it?'

'She hasn't. But would you like my advice, Angel?'

'Please.'

'If Leo Somerville's involved, then you should think carefully. Although I have to say I can't see Sam Richards being caught up in anything underhand. He's too up-front.'

'He did disappear without explanation when his career was riding high, and I can't help feeling it's all linked up.'

'You're going to have to speak to Sam if you want answers.'

'I won't be seeing him again.'

'Have you had a falling out?'

'There's no place for me in the new set-up. Park House has its own team of helpers.'

'Then what are you going to do?'

'I've come to a crossroads in my life. I suppose it's a question of choosing which way to go.'

'You're always welcome to stay with Lottie and me.'

'In your mobile home?' Bethany was forced into a reluctant smile.

'I shouldn't take Lottie too seriously on that one. She likes her creature comforts.'

'Maybe, but it's not the answer. I have to get a job, a proper one, and somewhere to live.'

'I suppose Canada is out of the question?'

'I can't run away again, although I know Ken and my mother would always welcome me.'

'Then you are in a fix,' Wendel agreed. 'But you know, I've always found things are never as bad as you think they are, and I've been in some tight spots in my time.'

Loud noises in the car park drew Wendel's attention outside. 'It seems the last of the bunch are moving off. Do you mind if I go and say goodbye to everyone?'

Wendel's appearance prompted a lot of laughter and good-natured banter. Bethany wished she possessed one half of his confidence, but no matter how she looked at things she couldn't share his optimism. Life had been different in Wendel's day. Scandals could be glossed over and in a short space of time everyone forgot about them. These days, with the world shrinking all the time, there was no such thing as a forgotten misdemeanour. What happened to Bethany would always be around to haunt her.

She decided there was no point in waiting for Leo Somerville to reappear. He was a busy man, and would probably be called back to London at short notice and completely forget all about her. As for Sam Richards, their paths would be unlikely to cross in the future.

Her mobile rang, disturbing her thoughts. 'Hi there,' Anthony greeted her. 'How are things with you?'

'Fine,' Bethany glossed over the truth.

'I hear you're not joining the new set-up?'

'It's time for me to move on.'

'That's a pity. What are you going to do now?'

'I haven't made any plans as such.'

'Have you spoken to Sam Richards?'

'He hasn't got anything for me.'

Doors slammed outside and vehicles hooted at each other as everyone began to drive out of the car park. 'What on earth's that racket?' Anthony demanded.

'Everyone's leaving.'

'Can I ask you a favour?'

'It depends what it is.'

'Will you promise to stay on at The Goose and Galleon until I've had a chance to talk to a few people?'

'How long for?'

'Leave it with me.' Anthony cut the call.

Wendel popped his head round the door. 'I'm going over to collect Bouncer. Someone's offered me a lift. I shouldn't be too long. Will you be all right on your own?'

Still trying to get her head together, Bethany assured him she would. With everyone gone, the house was eerily quiet. She hadn't been on her own in The Goose and Galleon before, and every little noise seemed to be magnified. She tried to concentrate on updating her CV. Every so often she could see reflected in her screen shadows of the trees bending under the weight of an unforgiving wind.

She had never been of a nervous disposition, but she couldn't shake off the feeling that something momentous was about to happen. She glanced at the ticking clock in the corner of the room. Its hands did not seem to have moved since she last looked.

In the distance she heard a vehicle slowing up outside. Headlights arced through the snug as a car drew into the car park. She heard the front door slam, then footsteps making their way down the corridor.

18

'The nerve of the man.' Wendel, accompanied by an overexcited Bouncer, strode into the snug, his hair blown on end from the strength of the wind.

'What did you say?' Bethany had to raise her voice against the background noise of Bouncer's barking.

'Bouncer, heel,' Wendel bellowed.

The terrier took no notice and continued greeting Bethany until she stooped down to pick him up and began fondling his ears. Squirming in delight, he stopped barking and settled contentedly in her arms.

'Sorry — didn't mean to spook you, Angel,' Wendel apologised.

'What's happened now?' Bethany asked with a weary sigh. 'Has Anthony Granger mistreated Bouncer?' The terrier gave a gentle bark at the mention of his name.

'It's Sam Richards who's upset me,'

Wendel snapped.

'Sam? What did he do?'

'He followed us into the car park.' The look of outrage on Wendel's face deepened.

Thoroughly confused, Bethany continued fondling Bouncer's ears, unsettled by the news that Sam was back.

'He was riding my bike. He's been using it as a runaround.'

'There's nothing wrong with that, is there?' Bethany queried.

'I'll nail him to the wall if he's upset all my fine-tuning.'

'He is a good rider,' Bethany said, attempting to calm her godfather down. 'And haven't you always said vehicles need to be used, not shut up in sheds?'

'I might've expressed an opinion of that nature,' Wendel mumbled, 'All the same, he should've asked permission first.'

'And how exactly was he supposed to get hold of you in your absence?'

'I'll thank you not to use that tone of voice with me.' Wendel frowned at her, an expression he often used when he knew he was in the wrong.

'You didn't leave a forwarding address.'

Wendel opened his mouth to speak, then closed it again.

'And,' Bethany warmed to her theme, 'if Sam hadn't ridden your bike while you were away, we wouldn't have been able to get to the fire in half the time we did.'

'You know how to kick a man when he's down, don't you?'

Bethany softened her voice. 'You're not down. But something else has upset you, hasn't it?'

'I don't like the idea of that man playing with your affections.'

'I beg your pardon?'

'I've been talking to some of the crew, and they seemed to think that he'd taken a shine to you.'

'A shine?' Bethany could feel laughter bubbling up inside her chest. 'What sort of talk is that?'

Wendel's mouth was set in a stubborn line. 'You've been through enough, and I won't have it.'

Bethany suddenly felt lighthearted. 'What's it to be, Wendel? Crash helmets at dawn?'

'You know what I mean. What was that for?' he demanded as Bethany leaned forward to kiss his cheek.

'For being you.' She smiled at him.

'Am I interrupting something?' Sam was now standing in the doorway, his dark brown hair glistening with drops of rain. He removed his leather jacket, revealing his logo-embossed T-shirt. Bethany's eyes were drawn to the vivid red dragon slashed across the front, its haughty head poised in dignified silence.

'Wendel was complaining that you used his bike without his permission,' she told him.

'Look, um ... ' Wendel was now busy sidling out of the door. 'Bouncer, heel.' The terrier wriggled out of Bethany's arms and trotted obediently across the floor towards Wendel, sniffing Sam's boots on the way. 'I'll leave you two alone. I'm sure you've loads of things you need to discuss. No harm done, Sam. Catch up with you later.' With exaggerated courtesy, Wendel closed the door gently behind him, leaving Bethany alone with Sam.

'Wendel did say I could use his bike whenever I wanted to,' Sam said. 'Sorry, I didn't think to ask.'

'Don't worry about Wendel.' Bethany strove to keep her voice steady. 'He's letting off steam. It's his way of showing how glad he is we're all in one piece after the events of the past few days.'

Sam had moved into the room and was now standing so close to Bethany she was finding it difficult to breathe. 'Did you forget something?' She took a step away from him.

'No.'

'Then what are you doing here?'

'I came to see you.'

'Why?'

'We have some unfinished business to discuss.'

'No we don't. You said goodbye.'

'Our unfinished business is of a personal nature. The last time I tried to get personal, we were interrupted by a newshound flashing his wretched camera in my face.'

'What is there left to say that hasn't already been said?' Bethany's breath was ragged and her cheeks were beginning to burn.

'Plenty,' Sam said with a teasing smile. 'Anthony Granger's been going round telling everyone I'm responsible for giving you the chop. He's busy drumming up support to have you reinstated, so I thought I'd better come on over and get things properly settled between us.'

'Properly settled?'

'We need to talk.'

'About what?'

'Us. The future.'

Bethany sank back into her chair. Sam followed her example and sat down opposite her.

'There is no us,' she insisted.

'I'd like to change that situation.'

'You've already explained that our

professional relationship is at an end. What else is there to discuss?'

'I understand you've been speaking to Leo Somerville?'

'If you've come to plead his case,' Bethany said, 'then I've already told him I'm not interested in anything he has to offer. I know he's promised that any new deal won't involve Harland, but it's a case of once bitten, twice shy.'

Sam frowned as if he were preoccupied with his own thoughts. The clock in the corner of the room ticked away a full minute.

'Sam?' Bethany prompted when he still didn't speak.

'I came back tonight because apart from anything Anthony has to say, I was afraid that if I left it until the morning, you might be gone.'

'Now Wendel's returned, and with a new wife, there's nothing to keep me here.'

Sam held up a hand to stop Bethany speaking. 'Three years ago I took a career break.'

'That's old news.'

'I was burnt out. The film world is intensive, and it can suck the life out of you. That's what it did to me. I was wrecked. I knew there was more to life than making films.'

'Sam, you don't have to explain any of this to me.'

'I took off, not sure where I was going; I only knew I had to get away. I had some idea of going back to nature. I eventually wound up in a small kingdom in Far Eastern Asia. The locals were naturally wary of accepting a stranger into their midst, but I think they recognised my need to de-stress. They let me stay on, and our days were filled with important but undemanding tasks. We worked from dawn to dusk drawing water from the well, building fires, growing vegetables and mending huts, fishing, that sort of thing. It was an idyllic existence.'

'Didn't you miss your old life?' Bethany couldn't resist asking the question.

'Occasionally, but not enough to make me want to return.'

'Then why did you?'

'For the money.'

Bethany's newfound respect for Sam evaporated in a flash. 'I'd forgotten how money plays such a big part in your life,' she said in a cold voice.

'This is where The Dragon comes in.' Sam smiled. 'So there's no need to look at me as though I were something particularly unpleasant that had crawled out from underneath a stone.' Bethany flushed. 'I'd probably have come to the same conclusion if I didn't know the full details.'

'What's The Dragon?' Bethany prompted.

'It's a foundation.'

'What does it do?'

'It was set up and financed by Leo Somerville.' Bethany stiffened at the mention of her old adversary's name. 'But I'm getting ahead of myself.'

A wild gust of wind outside rattled the windowpanes, and smoke billowed down the chimney and back into the room. Sam rose and kicked one of the logs back into place.

'Southeast Asia?' Bethany prompted after Sam sat down again.

'I should explain that I'd managed to learn enough of the local dialect to make myself understood in most situations. One day the village routine was thrown into disarray when a light aircraft came down not far from their settlement. There were two passengers on board — Leo and the pilot. Neither of them were injured, but they were in need of help. I translated to the village chief what had happened, and to cut a long story short, between us we mended their leaky fuel pipe and managed to get the aircraft going again.'

'Is that how you and Leo met?'

'Yes.'

Again Bethany waited for Sam to go on.

'As it was too dark to take off and the pilot wanted to do some tests before they flew again, they stayed over for a few days. While the pilot was sorting out the aircraft, Leo volunteered to help with the chores. We got talking and he explained he'd been on a fact-finding mission.'

'What sort of fact-finding mission?' Bethany asked.

'Has Leo ever mentioned his past to you?'

'Only the part about being given help by a powerful man when he was young.'

Sam nodded. 'He's tried to repay that debt over the years. I know that's not how he comes across, and you had every right not to trust him after the way he treated you.'

'He explained about that.' Bethany began to feel she might have seriously misjudged Leo Somerville.

'Anyway, Leo had been in that part of the world to see if he could do anything to help the plight of the underdeveloped regions. I explained they were a proud people and wouldn't take kindly to interference by an outsider.'

'They were right to object,' Bethany

agreed. 'Because they lead a different life to us it doesn't mean we have to impose our values on them.'

'I can see you and Leo are going to have some spirited discussions in the future.'

Bethany was too wound up to realise Sam had referred to their future together. 'So your little kingdom is happy as it is. Why change things?'

'Leo was impressed by everything the local people had done with regard to their settlement, but he could see that funds were needed to maintain essential services like health care, education, nutrition and . . . ' Sam paused. ' . . . equal rights.'

'Equal rights?'

'Women are treated well, but they're very much second-class citizens.'

'How can Leo Somerville possibly change that?'

'He doesn't want to, but he's been trying to make small changes.'

'Such as?'

'Do you agree that every child, male

or female, should be given an equal chance in life?'

'Yes, but it isn't always the case?'

'Exactly. Girl children are less valued and on occasions not always well treated. With the foundation's help, and in as sensitive a manner as possible, we're trying to change all that. We are gaining ground but it's slow. I wanted to be a part of Leo's plan, and I knew to do that I'd have to come back to the real world to raise our profile and frankly earn some money to put into the pot. I was mentally re-energised, and when Leo suggested *Love Will Find a Way* as a vehicle to re-establish my presence on the scene, I agreed.'

'Why does Harland Somerville have such a poor opinion of The Dragon?' Bethany asked.

'He doesn't.'

'That's not the impression he gave me.'

'That's because Leo doesn't want him involved in the business side of things. To put it bluntly, Harland would go down the wrong track. He isn't totally dishonest, but he's always striving to live up to his uncle's high standards.' Sam shrugged. 'And he hasn't got his uncle's business acumen. So Leo lets him run a small publicity side of the operation, seeing if he can persuade any of his friends to contribute to the foundation. We're not fashionable. We haven't been adopted by any celebrities, and we want to keep it that way.'

'Big names bring in the money,' Bethany pointed out.

'They can also rob a cause of its integrity. We were seeing a slow but steady success in the course of action we set out to achieve, but we've come up against a brick wall.'

'The authorities?'

'The villagers themselves.'

'Don't they like what you're doing for them?'

'On the contrary, they're right behind us. But Leo and I are both male, and they're beginning to register dissatisfaction with the fact that we have no female representative.'

'Are you suggesting I take on the role?'

'I can think of no better person.' Sam leaned forward, an eager smile on his face. 'Will you do it?'

'No.' Bethany shook her head.

'Why not?'

'Because you haven't told me everything.'

'What's Harland Somerville been saying?'

'He said if I knew the truth behind The Dragon and why you took off suddenly without a word to anyone, I might not be so ready to think well of you. He hinted at subterfuge.'

'There is no subterfuge,' Sam protested.

Bethany glanced down at the pale ring of flesh on the third finger of his left hand, then raised her eyes to meet Sam's. The look of unease that crossed his face confirmed her earlier suspicions. 'If you have nothing to hide, why haven't you told me about your wife?'

19

The wind whistling down the chimney-breast was the only sound to break the silence that had fallen between them.

'How did you find out?' Sam eventually asked.

Bethany screwed her tissue into a tight ball. 'I'm right aren't I?' she persisted. 'You have been married?'

Sam shifted position in his chair, looked into the fire and then back at Bethany.

'I'm not prying or anything,' she insisted.

'I know that, and I do owe you an explanation. But you haven't answered my question.'

Bethany took a deep breath. 'I could see you'd worn a ring at some time in your life from the pale band of flesh on your finger. It didn't take a degree in rocket science to work things out.'

Sam looked down at his hand, his face expressionless.

'Were you childhood sweethearts?' Bethany ventured to ask.

'We met at college.'

Sam's reluctance to speak made Bethany feel she was intruding on private ground, but she had to know about Sam's past if their relationship was to survive.

'I was a media arts student and Ranee worked for the catering company that ran the snack bar. One day there was a problem with the tea and coffee urns. I helped her sort it out, and in return Ranee offered me a free lunch. We got talking and she told me about her grandparents. They were Vietnamese boat people. The family had come over to this country in the seventies. Ranee was born here, but her cultural roots were in the old country.'

'If it hurts to talk about her, I understand,' Bethany said.

'You have to know everything,' Sam insisted, 'and now seems as good a time as any for us to talk.'

'If you're sure.'

After a few moments, Sam took up his story again. 'Ranee was a quiet girl. She didn't mix socially with the other students, but after the tea urn incident we took to sitting together of an evening when she'd finished her shift. We'd share a cup of coffee and talk about everything. Although she didn't like the bright lights, I sensed in her a twin soul. I told her of my hopes and dreams and she told me of hers. Gradually our feelings for each other deepened. Despite our different backgrounds, we decided to get married. I had no family, so there wasn't a problem on my side, but Ranee's parents were alive. We both knew I wasn't the type of husband they'd choose for their daughter, but we wanted to be together so much that Ranee was prepared to fly in the face of convention, even though my culture was different to hers and I'd never had a proper job in my life.' Sam gave a sad smile. 'Hardly a sound basis on which to start a marriage, but Ranee could be stubborn, and eventually her family came to accept that she wasn't going to change her mind and they welcomed me as their son-in-law. We grew to respect each other's values even if we didn't always agree. When I got my big career break and the chance to direct an important film, Ranee insisted I take it. I could tell she wasn't as happy as I was about the situation, but she didn't want to stand in my way. Are you with me so far?'

'Go on,' Bethany replied.

'I didn't pretend not to be married, like Anthony Granger, but Ranee was similar to Anthony's wife. She was publicity-shy. She hated the idea of attending galas or presentation ceremonies. Although I wore a wedding band, for some reason everyone assumed I was single. There was even a suggestion in one of the gossip mags that I pretended to be married and that was why I wore a ring.'

'You've told me all I need to know.'

Sam dismissed Bethany's words with a shake of his head. 'Ranee may not have sought the limelight, but she was a fervent supporter of female rights. Her grandmother had suffered badly as a young woman; she was married to a man who mistreated her, and when she ran away from him the family cut her off. I never knew the full details. It was never spoken of, and it wasn't my place to ask, but the incident fuelled Ranee's support for feminist issues.'

'I can understand why.'

'Although it wasn't a fashionable cause at the time, Ranee was passionate about feminism and its rightful place in society.'

'Was she very active?' Bethany asked.

'Not overtly, but we talked about setting up a foundation for young girls in her grandmother's situation. That was before I got my big break. I suppose I was so wrapped up in my work that my enthusiasm for the project got sidelined. That's why I didn't at first realise that something wasn't right with Ranee. By the time I learned there was more to her lack of enthusiasm for my career than mere mood swings, it was too late. Her leukaemia was too advanced for the doctors to do anything for her. Her parents never came to terms with their loss. She was their beloved only child and they couldn't live without her. They both passed on within the year, so in the space of twelve months I'd lost everyone I loved.' Sam ran his fingers through his hair. 'Now you know why I took off so suddenly and why I told no one the reason why.'

Knowing there were no words she could say, Bethany put her hand over Sam's and squeezed his fingers.

'I knew I had to do something in Ranee's memory, something she would respect. I chose the cause closest to her heart, and that's why I suggested to Leo that we set up The Dragon.'

'Does Leo know the reason behind your motivation?'

'I swore him to secrecy, but yes, he knows. He suggested calling the trust the Ranee Richards foundation, but I know she wouldn't have wanted that. In

Vietnamese folklore the dragon is regarded as a wise creature. He brings prosperity to the people, so The Dragon seemed a natural choice of name. Leo agreed with me.'

'Leo Somerville would appear to be a man of many surprises.'

'I know you've had issues with him, and that you want absolutely nothing to do with any project he's involved in, but I couldn't leave here without giving it one more try.'

'Giving what one more try?'

'Getting you to change your mind.'

'It means that much to you?' Bethany asked.

The hopeful light in Sam's eyes died. 'It did, but I realise it's expecting too much of you to take on such a commitment. I acted impulsively.'

'Is that the only reason you came back?'

Sam jerked his head upright. 'No it isn't,' he said firmly. 'You may as well hear the rest of my story.'

'There's more?'

'I suppose I'd fallen into the habit of not mentioning Ranee because I never expected to fall in love again. No, let me finish,' Sam stalled Bethany. 'If I keep going I might get all my confessions out in one go.' He expelled a quick breath, then started speaking again. 'From the moment I first saw you with your nose all red from drinking tomato soup, wearing a ridiculous hat, I knew you were special.'

'In what way?' Bethany asked in a shaky voice.

'You took my breath away. I mean there we were, invading your garden, it was snowing, and we were having a barbecue and dancing on Wendel's lawn, churning it up with our boots — and you never batted an eyelid.'

'I was in shock,' Bethany felt duty-bound to point out, 'and over the years I've learned that where Wendel is concerned, it's best not to make a fuss.'

'Talking of Wendel . . .'

'What about him?' Bethany asked in a resigned voice.

'I knew from the off he could be infuriating.'

'Most people do.' Bethany's face softened.

'Yet you never lost your cool with him.'

'That's because I can't help loving him. He's such an old rogue.'

'But there are times when he'd try the patience of a saint.'

'Nobody's perfect. Anyway, why were you so . . . ' Bethany struggled for the right word. ' . . . edgy?'

'Was I?' Sam looked perplexed.

'And that's a nice way of putting it.'

'I was probably annoyed at finding you looking so normal.'

'What was I supposed to look like?'

'I'd heard conflicting reports about you from Harland and Leo Somerville.'

'We always seem to come back to the Somervilles,' Bethany said in a flat voice.

'Leo's played a big part in all this.'

'How?'

'When the idea of a female representative for The Dragon was first raised,

Leo said he knew the ideal person for the job.'

'Are you saying I've been set up?'

'Not in so many words,' Sam hedged, 'but you really wouldn't reconsider your decision?'

In the distance they heard Bouncer barking at a vehicle driving into the car park. 'I'm not renowned for changing my mind,' Bethany said.

'I suppose you can't win them all.' Sam seemed to accept her decision as final. 'I'll tell Leo this was one he got wrong. I can't say I blame you, after all you've been through.' He looked round for his jacket.

'But on this occasion, I could be persuaded to make an exception,' Bethany said.

Sam was now searching in his pockets. 'Have you seen my keys?'

'Are you listening to me?'

'I've just remembered, I haven't got them on me. Do you think Wendel would let me borrow his bike again to get me back to Park House? One of the boys can bring it back later.'

'Sam.'

'What?' He blinked at Bethany, startled by her raised voice.

She was pleased to see she now had Sam's full attention. 'That's better. Now what we need is a few well-chosen celebrity names,' Bethany mused out loud, 'if we're really going to get things off the ground.'

Sam's look of confusion deepened.

'I'm sure Catriona Cleeve would be delighted to come on board. We could rope in Lottie to help with fundraising activities, although we'd need to keep an eye on her — she has a tendency to get carried away. But they're both strong female role models, and from different generations. They'd be ideal choices, don't you think?'

'You mean — what exactly do you mean?' Sam's surprise was reflected in his voice. 'Are you saying you're up for it?'

'Wasn't that what this meeting was all about?'

'Yes, but . . . ' Sam now looked lost for words. 'You're sure? I mean, after all you said about Leo Somerville? Have you changed your mind?'

'I'm looking for a job and you've offered me one.'

'It's important you fully understand the situation.'

'I think you've explained everything.'

'It won't be easy,' Sam warned her. 'Out in the field the conditions can be basic. I can't offer to pay you much. We'd be separated for long periods and on occasions living in different parts of the world. Communication isn't reliable and you could be cut off for days.'

'If something's worth doing then sacrifices have to be made, wouldn't you say?'

Sam looked as though a great truth had been revealed to him. 'Leo Somerville was right about you all along.'

'We need to talk about him,' Bethany began.

Sam made a sudden gesture with his hands at the sound of a disturbance in the corridor. 'Can it wait? Only I think I can hear Lottie approaching.'

'Oh no.' Bethany sat bolt upright.

'Don't say anything about anything until I've had a chance to talk to Leo first,' Sam implored. 'If Lottie gets wind of what's going on, the news will go viral in nanoseconds.' He snatched up his leather jacket.

'Where are you going?' Bethany asked.

'I need to catch Leo before he takes off for London.'

'We haven't finished here.'

'You're not going to back out now, are you?' All the warmth left Sam's face.

'Haven't you forgotten something?' Bethany crossed her arms and waited patiently for Sam's reply.

'I don't think so.' Sam looked puzzled.

'By what title are you going to introduce me to your villagers?'

His face cleared. 'You can choose one,' he said. 'I'm sure they won't mind what you call yourself.'

'I quite like the sound of Mrs Richards.'

'You can't do that unless we . . . ' Sam's voice tailed off. ' . . . get married.'

'You don't think that's a good idea?'

'But I thought . . . ' For the first time since Bethany had known him, Sam looked unsure of himself. 'I mean, my wife?'

'Why not? You've admitted you're in love with me, or did I get that wrong?'

'Are you . . . I mean, do you feel the same about me?' Sam asked with a hesitant smile.

'If you're asking if I'm in love with you, then I have to say I have been from the moment you thrust your wretched mobile phone at me,' Bethany admitted, 'though goodness knows why. It's been the bane of my life ever since.'

'Then throw it away.'

'Did you know I actually cut off one of Leo Somerville's calls?'

'I'm fed up with talking about the

Somervilles,' Sam said.

'Me too.'

The door behind Sam opened. 'There you are, darlings. Have you seen Wendel anywhere?' Lottie's green eyes gleamed as she assessed the situation in front of her. 'Am I interrupting anything?' she asked with an arch note in her voice.

'Yes, I am about to propose marriage to Bethany,' Sam replied in a calm voice.

Lottie's face lit up. 'Wendel,' she called over her shoulder, 'did you hear that? Sam and Bethany are going to get married. Isn't it too marvellous? Leave all the arrangements to me, darlings. Wendel,' she called again, raising her voice, 'where are you? Oh, never mind, we don't need him.'

'We don't actually need you at this moment either, Lottie,' Bethany pointed out gently.

'I'm in the way?' Lottie looked surprised. It wasn't often she was asked to leave a room. 'You're right,' she said, recovering her good nature, 'of course you don't want me right now. I'll make myself scarce.'

'I'd prefer to say what I have to say to Sam in private,' Bethany agreed.

Lottie put a horrified hand to her mouth. 'You aren't going to turn him down, are you, darling?'

'Isn't that what the Dowager Duchess de Montchapelle advised her prospective daughter-in-law to do?'

'Stuff that,' was Lottie's robust reply. 'My advice is take him before he changes his mind. Look at the trouble I had getting Wendel to commit. Sam, you get on with proposing while I go and track down Wendel. Where is the wretched man?'

'You haven't much time,' Bethany urged Sam as Lottie left the door open behind her. 'I think I heard the pop of a champagne cork. Wendel's been listening in.'

'Guilty as charged.' Wendel appeared in the doorway holding a tray of drinks. 'Would you like the bike as a wedding present, Sam? It's awfully good at going over rough terrain. And if you get stuck, Bethany knows how to carry out a basic service, a skill that should come in more than useful in primitive parts of the world.'

'Bethany,' Sam urged, 'quick, before we get any more interruptions. Will you marry me?'

The snug fell silent. Bethany smiled at Sam. 'I will,' she said in a voice that was little more than a whisper.

In one stride Sam crossed the room and enveloped her in his arms; and, not caring that both Wendel and Lottie were looking on, kissed her.

'Now that's what I call a wrap,' Lottie said with an approving smile.

We do hope that you have enjoyed reading this large print book.

Did you know that all of our titles are available for purchase?

We publish a wide range of high quality large print books including:
Romances, Mysteries, Classics
General Fiction
Non Fiction and Westerns

Special interest titles available in large print are:
The Little Oxford Dictionary
Music Book, Song Book
Hymn Book, Service Book

Also available from us courtesy of Oxford University Press:
Young Readers' Dictionary
(large print edition)
Young Readers' Thesaurus
(large print edition)

For further information or a free brochure, please contact us at:
Ulverscroft Large Print Books Ltd.,
The Green, Bradgate Road, Anstey,
Leicester, LE7 7FU, England.
Tel: (00 44) **0116 236 4325**
Fax: (00 44) **0116 234 0205**

THE ROSE AND THE REBEL

Valerie Holmes

In stifling summer heat, Miss Penelope
Rose decides to take a swim — scan-
dalously, in an outdoor pool on her
father's estate. Having sent off her
maid, Penelope strips to her under-
clothes and indulges herself in the
coolness of the secluded water. But
when she climbs out, wearing only
her soaked chemise, her dress has
disappeared! To make matters con-
siderably more embarrassing, she
finds herself standing face to face
with the culprit — Mr Lucas Bleakly,
the eligible bachelor son of the local
reverend . . .

AS THE FOUR WINDS BLOW

June Davies

Isobel Blundell isn't looking forward to her special birthday. Her archaeologist husband, Douglas, is in South America, and she and their three children miss him sorely. On her birthday, Isobel's mother Ailsa, and sisters Kirsty and Dorrie, give her Douglas's gift — an airline ticket! Overjoyed, Isobel sets off for a holiday with him at the dig. But heartache, danger, conflict and tragedy lie ahead for the whole family — those at home, as well as Isobel and Douglas in South America.

THE INHERITANCE

Wendy Kremer

Sara expects that when a local group of people from her village who want a say in the future of an empty manor house confront the new owners, her own loyalty will be clear and simple — but that's before she is unexpectedly chosen to talk things over with the new owner, Madame Jannet Rogard, and her attractive son, Nick, at their ch<tåteau in France. What's more, even though Sara and Nick come from different worlds, there's no denying the attraction growing between them . . .

KILTS AND HIDDEN CRUSHES

Judy Jarvie

Café owner Callie Dewar finds the return of her teenage crush too hot to handle. Hamish Gordon is back in St. Andrews, volunteering as a waiter while secretly yearning to rekindle the spark that's been smouldering between them. Then pair are unwittingly brought together for a holiday in the Highlands — but Callie is harbouring a deep secret that she dare not share with anyone, least of all Hamish. Will she succeed in pushing her hunky ex-flame away? Or will kilted chemistry, family trickery, and an errant sheep change their destinies?